O

KENTUCKY KILLER

The end of America's bloody Civil War should have brought peace to the land. It didn't, and — like countless others — the Weilocks, a family of German immigrants, lost everything. The lone survivor, Gunter, promises to make Jonathon Gates, the leader of the bushwhackers who murdered his family, pay for his crimes. But the bushwhackers have become masters of guerrilla warfare and seem unbeatable. Would Gunter's burning desire for revenge be enough to even the odds? Only time — and hot lead — would tell.

DEREK TAYLOR

KENTUCKY KILLER

Complete and Unabridged

LINFORD
Leicester

First published in Great Britain in 2001 by
Robert Hale Limited
London

First Linford Edition
published 2002
by arrangement with
Robert Hale Limited
London

British Library CIP Data

Taylor, Derek
   Kentucky killer.—Large print ed.—
Linford western library
1. Western stories
2. Large type books
I. Title
823.9'14 [F]

ISBN 0–7089–9885–2

Published by
F. A. Thorpe (Publishing)
Anstey, Leicestershire

Set by Words & Graphics Ltd.
Anstey, Leicestershire
Printed and bound in Great Britain by
T. J. International Ltd., Padstow, Cornwall

This book is printed on acid-free paper

For Helena with a fond 'Hello'.

1

Jed Brand burst through the batwings of the Single Spur Saloon and fired into the air. A sudden silence gripped the place. Jed Brand was not unknown to the citizens of Butcher's Town; he was, after all, their sheriff. But he was not much given to dramatic gestures of this kind and people knew that if he was trying to attract their attention in such a way there had to be a good reason for it. When he'd got the silence he reckoned so solemn an announcement as the one he was about to make deserved, he declared: 'The war's over. Union's won, but the war is over.'

The silence continued for a moment while a range of emotions flowed around the smoky, beery atmosphere of the saloon and good-time gals collected themselves. Then suddenly the air filled with a raucous cheering. Winners or losers, the war was over. Those who'd survived it had not been butchered or killed by it; this was cause enough for celebration. The losing part of it was something that could be dealt with later.

Not everyone in and around Butcher's Town received the news of the Civil War's end with such relief. A good few of them vowed to carry it on where and however they could.

'We ain't been fighting Davis' war, anyway,' spat out Jonathon Gates, who'd been chewing on the remains of a plug of tobacco. 'We's been fighting our own war. And that's what I aim to do, carry on fighting it.'

And to prove it he and a band of a dozen men he led, all the dispossessed sons of wealthy landowners who'd lost all to roving Union Regulars, rode on to a farm owned by known Union sympathizers to take as much revenge as they could. They were mounted on fine breeds, even if some of them were not as well groomed as they should be, and they were armed to the teeth with an arsenal of old and new weapons, many of them stolen from Union soldiers they'd slaughtered in guerrilla style attacks.

Folk on the Weilock spread were no longer on their guard against attacks from bushwhackers; instead they were indoors celebrating the end of a long and nasty war by downing pint after pint of good ol' home-brewed German beer. Jonathon Gates and his men did not know this and approached the spread cautiously. Making their way through the thick woods that surrounded the Weilock farm, they were surprised not to have to deal with any look-outs. Through the sound of wind and birds in the trees, they began to hear music and song and laughter.

'Sounds to me like they already think themselves saved,' Gates remarked.

'That's mighty careless,' said a man who'd remained at Gates's side throughout the whole conflict. They'd saved one another's skins on numerous occasions and were thought by many to lead a charmed existence, at least as far as bullets and cannon fire was concerned.

'I'd say so,' Gates agreed.

'Well, what d'you think?' Billy Taylor asked, sitting up tall in his saddle and fingering a Colt Model 1851 Navy revolver that was stuck into the belt of his breeches just behind the buckle. It was only one of six loaded guns he kept about his person. He was twenty-six years old but had lost count of the number of men he had sent to meet their Confederate-bashing maker.

'Never did like the sound of German beer songs. It always struck me they was boastful somehow.'

'Never liked Germans, full stop,' Billy Taylor said.

They were not speaking in hushed voices, since there was evidently no need, and the men spread around them heard their talk and muttered amongst themselves in agreement.

'Like some of their women, though,'

one was heard to remark in lascivious tones. Some of the others sniggered rudely in agreement.

'Well,' said Jonathon Gates, looking at his trusty sidekick, 'let's go gatecrash the party, then.'

As he said it he spurred his horse into a trot to cut a path through the trees, reining to the left and then to the right. Taylor and the others followed him, their long hair and flaps of clothing lifting in the wind. They might have looked a romantically daring, bush-whacking crew did they not have bloodletting on their minds. Much to their cost, no one on the Weilock spread heard them coming, despite the piercing sound of their rebel yells.

More drunk than anyone of the Weilock household that evening was Gunter Weilock. At twenty-six, he was the eldest of the Weilock's six children and, like his father, pro-abolitionist. It was often remarked upon that to be a Weilock slave was to be very lucky indeed. Even now, the Weilock blacks, free for years, were all indoors drinking to the Union victory around the table with the Weilock family.

Gunter, who had the instincts of a natural born survivor, mid-chorus of a particularly rousing German beer song, suddenly felt that something was not right. He got up from the table and went to peer out of a window. As he did so Jonathon Gates's bunch of bush-whackers suddenly opened fire on the house. As windowpanes shattered and wall timbers splintered, a wave of panic spread through the family. They jumped up from the table, the women rushing to pull the children to the floor, the men, sobering up on the instant, rushing to get their guns. Wilhelm Weilock, father of Gunter, saw little of the bloody battle that ensued. The first to die, he was hit in the neck by a bullet that severed his jugular vein and lodged in his windpipe. No one saw it happen. The impact of the bullet spun him around and he fell to the floor. As he lay dying a bullet from Gunter's Le

Mat carbine had already done for one of Gates's men.

Gunter's brothers were also now at windows, firing into the dark. Their mother Alix had all their wives and children collected under the large dining table and was shielding them with her body. The noise of gunfire and wood splintering coupled with the din of horses whinnying and rebel yells filled the air. In the dim light of paraffin-lamps her eyes darted all about the room. She could see her sons and they were all still standing, but where was Wilhelm? Then she saw him lying on the ground, a hand clutching his throat. She was torn between shielding her family and running to him. Then suddenly her youngest was sent reeling backwards from the window he was firing out of. This was her worst nightmare. Surely the war was over. Why was this happening? Without another thought she ran to her husband.

'Wilhelm, Wilhelm!' she shrieked,

shaking him but seeing no life in the eyes that stared up at her. Next she ran to her youngest. He, too, was dying, from a bullet in the chest. Then another son was hit. And another. And another.

Gunter could not fail but to see what was happening. '*Mein Gott*, no!' he cried out loud. He turned back to the window and fired more rapidly at the men who were besieging the house. One of his bullets rammed home into the guts of one of Gates's men. That made three down. Suddenly his carbine was out of ammunition. As he turned to reload it he saw a bullet hit his mother. She fell sprawled across his middle brother. He ran to her but she was dead before he got to her. In a mixture of blind panic and rage he looked at the women and children cowering under the table. They were all going to be killed, he could see it.

Outside Gates and Taylor, seemingly as immune to gunfire as ever, continued to lead what was left of their men in sending a never-ending hail of lead into the Weilocks' cabin. They were loving every minute of it, full of a terrible conviction that they were taking revenge for all the murder and mayhem the North had wreaked upon the South. They had known the Weilocks but had never thought of them as neighbours. The Weilocks and all the German immigrants, for that matter, had kept themselves too much to themselves to ever be thought of as that. And then, when the row over slavery had reached full crescendo and the Weilocks had taken the wrong side, they'd put themselves beyond the pale. This was their punishment. A punishment that had to be finally meted out to them for simply being different, and now particularly for being on the winning side.

'Fire,' Taylor called to Gates. 'Let's burn 'em out!'

This seemed like a wonderful idea to Gates and he signalled agreement to his sidekick, who then went about making fire and putting it in the places where it would most effectively take hold. Inside the farmhouse, Gunter, a few Negroes and his last surviving brother kept up as much gunfire as they were able. They weren't hitting any more of their attackers though and were losing the battle. Gunter's brain was working nineteen to the dozen trying to think of a way of saving the women and the children. Then he had it. Surrender. They would have to surrender and throw themselves on the mercy of the Confederates. His thoughts had only just finished forming themselves when the smell of smoke filled his nostrils. Oh no, not that! he thought to himself.

'We're gonna have to surrender,' he called out to his brother and the Negroes. 'Otherwise, they're all gonna die,' he added, pointing to the women and children, who were still cowering under the table.

Johann, his brother, agreed with him; the Negroes, too, all knowing they were doomed to die in an inferno otherwise.

'We're coming out,' Gunter's powerful voice called out to the rebels. He didn't know if he could trust the rebels or not, but he just hoped they had not yet gone so far beyond what was expected in a civilized world as to open fire on women and children.

Gates heard Gunter's words over the din of the gunfire and he called his men to cease firing. The roof of the farmhouse was beginning to blaze as what was left of the Weilock family began to file out and hurry down the steps of the farmhouse into the midst of Gates's gang. Gates might have let them be had his eyes not fallen on the Negroes amongst them. Any compassion he might have felt for the Weilocks suddenly evaporated in the heat of his hatred of the black race that had so bedevilled his world. Gunter, who'd kept guard at a window to cover his family lest the rebels should prove more savage than they'd already been, sensed what was going to happen next. Gates was not in his sights but Taylor was and

11

Taylor always took his lead from Gates.

'*Ja!*' Gates suddenly shrieked in bloodcurdling tones.

This was all the indication of what to do next that Taylor needed. Letting out his own yell, he raised his gun and began to close his finger around the trigger. The shot he fired went wide as a slug from Gunter's carbine smashed into his chest, throwing his arms wide and knocking him from his horse. Gates gasped as he saw his sidekick of so many battles fall. It shattered his belief in their invincibility, and it enraged him. In a frenzy of despair and blind panic he turned his guns on the Weilock group as it huddled together pathetically before him. His men did likewise.

'No! No!' Gunter screamed. 'No! No!'

He fired his carbine until there were no bullets remaining to discharge. He left none of Gates's men living, as they had left none of his family alive. Gates had firepower aplenty still but as all around him fell silent he ceased his firing. The farmhouse by now was a raging inferno. In its light Gunter saw his aggressor lit up as if by the sun. At last he looked to his own safety and hurried away from what had once been his happy home, swearing as he went to make Jonathon Gates pay for the wrong he had done.

2

All was quiet in Butcher's Town as Sheriff Jed Brand made his way down Main Street to his office. There had been two days and nights of merrymaking and now people would start to come back down to earth. Brand wondered how long it would be before Union soldiers arrived to occupy the town and the county. Wondered how long it would be before the South was finally subdued enough to satisfy the Northern victors that it was the vanquished.

A mist hung over everything as Brand made his way along Main Street. It was just gone six in the morning. There had been many Union sympathizers in the county, especially amongst those of German extraction. Kentucky had for some reason attracted Germans like a magnet and they had thought Lincoln and the abolitionists were right. He guessed that now they'd become favourites with the occupying forces. That would not go down well in the county. He smelled trouble ahead. Law-keeping in these parts was not going to be easy for a while.

He cooked himself some bacon and beans and washed it all down with coffee. It was still only half past seven. He looked out of his office window, drinking a second mug of coffee. The town was coming alive. He guessed some of the men from the county who'd joined the Kentucky Ninth Infantry must have survived. They'd be coming home. But to what?

Gunter Weilock knew. Paralysed by the trauma of it all, he had watched Jonathon Gates ride away out of the light thrown by the raging inferno that was consuming what had only shortly before been his family's home and into the darkness of the night. Then he had walked to where his wife, his children, his sister, sisters-in-law and their children all lay dead, the Negroes amongst them. He separated the bodies and laid each one out beside the other. His parents and his brothers were at that moment being cremated in the burning timbers of the house. The thought made him drop to his knees. The whole family had been good Lutherans; he supposed he ought to pray.

The Weilocks' nearest neighbours were some way off but by dawn they knew something terrible had happened to them. As the morning mists began to rise, friendly arms were put around Gunter and he was led away. He remained in a state of shock for a number of days, during which time the dead were buried, his family with due ceremony, Gates's gang without any. The whole town turned out for the funerals of the Weilocks and no greater show of sympathy could have been forthcoming. When it was over Gunter began to come to his senses. He had been staying with friends but now he decided he wanted to return to the farm. Their barns were still standing and in one of them he decided to make himself a home. Sheriff Brand rode with him the day he returned.

'It's a terrible thing that has happened, Gunter, and I shall not rest until I have hunted down Gates, though there's been no sight of him anywheres in these parts,' he said to Gunter as they rode on to the farm, adding, 'I know it's hard for you, son, but I don't want you riding out after him. The war was over and he will have known it. Now he's just an outlaw and should be dealt with as such. You go trying to hunt him down and there's no telling what might happen. The Union soldiers will be here any day now and then there'll be nowhere he can hide. He'll be hunted down like a wild animal and, if they get him alive, he'll be put on trial and hung.'

Gunter said nothing in reply to Brand. Brand was of English extraction and open as a book. He knew the

Germans to be taciturn and did not try to elicit from Gunter an indication of how he was feeling. And when Gunter began to organize a home for himself in the smallest of the barns and was still not saying very much, he decided it was time he left. He told him he'd drop by in a few days to see how he was. Getting no reply, he swung up on his horse and rode off back to town. A week later word reached town that Gunter was no longer on the farm and that nobody knew where he'd gone.

* * *

Jonathon Gates cared nothing about what had happened to the Weilocks. They were Union sympathizers, they got what they deserved. What he did feel bad about was the loss of his men, and of Taylor in particular. But that was war. He soon got over it. Three days later and he'd ridden East and found another band of men, men to whom he was well known, to make his own. Their leader was a man called Chandler.

'It's over,' Chandler replied to the suggestion made by Gates that they turn their attentions now to harrying the Union forces as they tried to occupy the South.

'Who says?' was Gates's answer.

They were deep in a wood sitting around a campfire in the early evening.

'I ain't licking no Union boots. The South is ours, with or without slaves,' a youth of nineteen snarled. Studying him, Gates could see he was just the sort he wanted now on his side.

'Yeah,' said another. 'What's there left for us now anyway, but to fight on?'

'Your families,' was Chandler's answer. 'Go home. Go back to your farms and plantations and rebuild them. Your families will need you.'

None of the men gathered around the campfire were prepared to see the sense in what he said. Not when Jonathon Gates was in their midst, egging them on to perpetuate the kind of thrillingly dangerous lives they'd grown used to.

'You go, Chandler,' Gates said. 'No one would blame you for doing so. But for me, and anyone who wants to join me, there's still plenty of work to do to make sure this so called peace ain't gonna be nothing of the sort for the Union armies that try and take hold of Kentucky.'

'You'll all die,' Chandler remarked. 'And haven't enough died already?'

'Not nearly enough Yankees,' sneered the youth who had first caught Gates's eye.

Throwing a quick glance Gates's way, the youth hoped he was making the right impression. The kind of look Gates returned reassured the youth and all the other men gathered around. And when Chandler rode out of the camp the next morning he did so with just a handful of the sixty or more irregulars that had made up his company, many of whom had ridden with him through the long years of the War Between the

States. The rest stayed to ride with Gates.

Amongst them was a woman, pretty as anything but respected and left alone by the men.

'Who's she?' Gates asked the youth who'd caught his eye.

'That's Charlotte Jones,' he replied. His name was Jake Mahon. He was five foot eight inches tall, with long black flowing hair and almost white skin. 'Her whole family were killed when Union soldiers overran their farm. She hid under a bed for three days and then the devils moved on. Been with us about a year.'

'She sure is pretty. She spoken for by anyone?' Gates enquired.

'No, nor ain't she gonna be,' Mahon replied, the tone of his voice full of telling but affectionately humorous with it.

'Is that so?' mused Gates, imagining himself at some time in the near future getting to know her whether she liked it or not. For this reason and this reason alone he let her ride with them. Otherwise, despite the upheavals wrought by the war, he thought a woman's place was at home by the hearth tending to the needs of her family.

'We riding today?' Mahon asked him, wanting to change the subject.

'Ain't no point in hanging about here, son,' Gates replied. 'Besides, North's gotta be taught a lesson. This war ain't over 'til it's over, which means, we got a lot of hunting and harrying to do.'

3

Gunter Weilock had found it impossible to stay put on what had been the family farm. He had lost his whole family, immediate and otherwise, to Confederate bushwhackers and something had to be done about it. For three days he had tried to create a new home for himself in the barn, but his nerves had got the better of him and he'd achieved nothing. Neighbours and friends had dropped in on him but their soothing words had not consoled him and their remarks that the law would bring Jonathon Gates to book had at first exasperated him and then incensed him. So he saddled up his favourite steed and rode.

He had some idea of where the bushwhackers had hung out and headed East in that direction. An eerie calm seemed to hang over the land.

Along the main trails there were wagons and riders going places. Maybe home, or away from it, to start new lives or return to the old. Here and there was a company of Union soldiers, getting ready, it seemed, to take up managing the peace somewheres round about. The sight of it all only served to deepen Gunter's hurt and whenever he could he rode off the trail and made his way through open countryside.

Getting near dusk on the second day he came across a group of people camped in a spinney. He was, as he usually did, going to give it a wide berth when he heard the sound of what he knew to be German speakers. Reining in his horse and dismounting, he took cover behind a large cottonwood. Then, drawing nearer, he could hear quite clearly that the voices were indeed speaking German. As he listened to hear what they were saying, he heard one he thought he recognized. Could it be? Was that Hans, a friend of his youth, who, rumour had it, had gone

24

North to enlist as a Yankee regular? He was an only son and almost in the first month of the war his father had been killed in a saloon in Butcher's Town for criticizing the Confederate president Jefferson Davis for getting them into a conflict they couldn't hope to win. He had fled under cover of night and had not been heard from since. Gunter became convinced it was him and drew closer to the group. Whatever, he knew they were not Confederates or Confederate sympathizers and he decided he could risk making an open approach.

With reins in hand and his horse walking behind him, he strolled into the camp. The camp was all bustle and no one challenged him. Casting an eye about, his gaze at last fell on a face that he knew definitely to belong to his old school friend. He tied up his horse to the slim branch of a tree, and began to walk towards the little group of comrades whom his friend, Hans Kung, somehow or other was managing to make laugh.

'Hans, Hans Kung, is that you?' he asked when he was almost on top of the group.

Hearing Gunter's voice over the laughter and chatter of his comrades, Hans turned to see who it was. He was sitting with his back against a tree.

'Who's asking?' he queried, casually turning to see who it was.

Gunter said nothing at first, waiting to see if his old friend recognized him.

'Gunter?' Hans said at last, beginning to get to his feet. 'Is that you?'

'It is, Hans. And I thought I recognized your voice.'

As war makes men who have survived a terrible conflict do, they embraced like long-lost brothers.

'But what brings you here?' Hans asked, standing back and looking at his friend to see in what shape he was after all this time. 'I heard you had stayed at home and worked the farm.'

The mention of the farm caused the colour to drain from Gunter's face.

It was replaced with a look of abject sorrow.

'Oh no!' Hans said. 'Don't tell me something terrible has happened to your family. Don't tell me that.'

But he knew that it had, though the cruelty of what he was told by Gunter shocked even him, a hardened veteran of a terrible civil war.

'You say you know who did it?' Hans remarked to Gunter after a long silence in which both men pictured the loving family that had been so mercilessly slaughtered. Hans remembered his own loving father, also a victim of the War Between the States.

'Yes,' said Gunter. 'It was a bushwhacker named Jonathon Gates. He and his sidekick have been running riot all over for years. People were saying they were immune to bullets but we proved they weren't and killed them all bar Gates himself. I saw his face as clear as daylight. I'd know him anywhere.'

'And you were going after him alone?'

'What else, Hans? You know we Germans have tried to avoid getting involved in this war. You know whose side we were on, but we had our farms and families to protect. That's all changed for me now. Maybe too late, but it's changed. But I couldn't expect the others to help me hunt down Gates. It's my battle.'

'The war was always gonna come to you, Gunter. That's what has been so terrible about it. And it's never gonna be over. As long as the South has a breath in its body, it's never gonna be over.'

'No,' agreed Gunter, thinking that it couldn't be over for him until Gates was dead.

Hans could sense what he was thinking. 'You can't do it alone, Gunter. This man Gates will already have gathered other men around him. It's obvious that he and all the bushwhackers intend to carry on the war. That's why we're here. Me and my men. Our orders are to flush them out. Join us,

Gunter, and we'll get Gates and he will pay for what he's done.'

Gunter knew there was a lot of sense in what Hans was saying. He couldn't go it alone. Or if he did he was more likely than not the one who would get killed, not Gates. He was good with a gun, but not that good. And unlike Gates, or Hans, for that matter, he had not cut his teeth in the bloody ground of this war that had raged for nigh on four years.

'All right,' he said. 'But I want to get him, Hans. I've gotta get him. I've gotta be the one. It's gotta be me.'

'You betcha,' said a relieved Hans, putting his arm around his old friend's shoulders. 'You betcha.'

*   *   *

Early the next morning, in a small town not far away, Jonathon Gates and his men were riding into town seeking food and drink. When the townsfolk saw them coming trotting down Main

Street they cringed. The war was over but these men riding in could only mean trouble. To a man the town had been solidly Confederate but they were happy to breathe a sigh of relief and to move on. Maybe now men would start paying for the things they sought, instead of presuming to take them in the name of the war effort. So they had been thinking for a week but now these men had ridden in to town.

They pulled up outside the town's saloon, dismounted and tied their horses to a hitching rail. They were all thirsty and looking forward to wetting their craws with a beer, excepting it was early in the morning and the saloon was closed. Stepping up to the saloon's batwings, Gates opened them to expose a glass-windowed door, which he knocked upon. When no one came immediately to answer, he knocked again, saying:

'Seems like folk round here don't know how to be hospitable.'

'It sure looks that way,' agreed

Mahon, who'd taken up a position beside him while the rest of the men were spread out along the plankwalk.

Still getting no reply, Gates began impatiently to turn the door handle. Then, suddenly stepping back and drawing his gun, he shot out the lock.

'All right, all right!' a voice mixed with impatience and horror called out from within. It was the barkeep pulling up his braces as he rushed to answer the door. 'What the hell do you think you're playing at? You don't have to go wrecking the door,' he reproached, stopping short as he came face to face with Gates.

'You didn't have to go locking it,' was Gates's snarled reply.

Pushing past him and before he could make a reply, Gates ordered the barkeep to get behind the bar and get him and his men something to quench the terrible thirst they had on them. The barkeep didn't like it. He was well used to handling trouble but he could see that the drink these men were surely going to consume was going to cost him dear. But, still, if he didn't want his place wrecked, he knew he was going to have to be compliant in meeting their demands.

'What y'all drinking?' he asked, taking an apron thrown on the counter from the night before and putting it on.

'Beer,' was Gates's reply.

'Think I'll go find a hotel and have myself a bath,' said the woman whom Gates had asked Mahon about.

The sound of a female voice surprised the barkeep and he looked up to see from whom amongst these bushwhacking characters so pretty-sounding a thing belonged to. Charlotte Jones, or Lottie as the men had grown accustomed to calling her, didn't look to him any different from the others.

'You a woman?' he asked incredulously.

'Well, she ain't no other kind of breed,' Gates roared, thinking he had cracked a joke the others would share with him. But he didn't reckon on

Lottie having gained the kind of respect you get when you've shared the hardships of a tough life on the trail and shown yourself to be every bit as equal to them as the next man. Getting no audience response to his remark and to hide his embarrassment, he tried to take the joke further by adding: 'Sure thing. You go have your bath and maybe I'll come along later and join you.'

Respecting Gates for his reputation as one of Kentucky's most feared bushwhackers and not wanting Mahon or anyone thinking they had to rush to save her blushes, Lottie felt willing to put up with Gates's drunken ribaldry and gave him back as good as he gave, saying, 'You jump in any bath and the water's likely to jump out.'

This made the men laugh. 'I'll bathe on my own, thanks,' she continued, walking up to the shattered saloon door. Then she turned to say to the general gathering, 'but when you decide to leave town you be sure and let me know.'

'Don't worry, Lottie, we ain't going nowhere without you,' Mahon answered for all of them.

'Something going on between you two?' Gates asked, as Lottie went through the batwing doors.

'No,' replied Mahon, 'I, well, we just naturally, well, kinda always look out for her.'

'Hmm!' Gates replied disdainfully, taking hold of the glass of beer in front of him, emptying what was left in one swallow and slapping it down on the counter. It told the barkeep he wanted another. Gates said nothing more about Lottie but had some dark thoughts about the women in the war he'd had one way or another, whether they had wanted it or not. A snigger spread across his face but the barkeep, seeing it as he brought him another frothing beer, would not have had the least idea of what it was about.

An hour or so of steady drinking ensued before Gates suddenly began to feel hungry.

'Barkeep,' he demanded suddenly, 'you got ham 'n' eggs?'

'Not here, but you can get them at the hotel.'

'But I ain't at the hotel down the road,' Gates replied. 'I'm here and I don't feel much like moving. Do any of you?' he asked his men, all of whom, taking their lead from him, replied in similarly oafish ways that they did not.

The barkeep didn't quite know how to respond. He wished the town had a sheriff but it didn't. He had gone off to investigate some lawlessness out of town three or four months ago and had not yet returned. It was assumed he was dead somewhere. The job had been offered around but no one had wanted it. Manpower was short in the county, because of the war.

'Well?' demanded Gates, belching loudly, his stomach feeling very acid.

'I don't know exactly,' the barkeep replied. 'We ain't ever served food in this saloon before.'

Gates, getting impatient, was beginning to feel an inclination to shoot up the place, when a rider came storming into town, near falling off his horse outside the saloon in his haste to deliver his message. Gates's hand was on his gun, when the rider burst into the saloon.

'Union soldiers about two miles out of town, Mr Gates,' the rider, who was known to the men inside as Longshanks on account of being so tall and riding a short horse, gasped between catching his breath. He had been left some distance out of town to keep look-out.

Gates showed no immediate reaction, though Mahon and the others sat up.

'Regulars or irregulars?' Gates asked after a moment's reflection.

'Regulars, I reckon, though I didn't hang around to look too closely. I seed they was not friendly-looking and took off for here.'

Again Gates seemed not to be unduly concerned.

'Well,' he said, turning to the

barkeep. 'Are we gonna get those ham 'n' eggs or not?'

When the barkeep seemed lost for an answer, Gates suddenly pulled his gun and shot to bits a splendid mirror that had adorned the rear wall of the bar. This was a signal to his men to start doing likewise. As slugs began to fly all round the saloon, the barkeep dived under the counter. Longshanks took the opportunity to grab a glass of beer from a table to slake his thirst. The barkeep had a shotgun on a shelf under the counter but thought better of using it and so while he took cover and Longshanks supped beer a tempest of lead reduced the saloon to a shattered and splintered wreck. It was all over in a few minutes and as Gates holstered his gun, he leant over the counter and looked down at the cowering barkeep and asked, 'Where d'you say we could get those ham 'n' eggs?'

'Jonathon,' Mahon interrupted him, 'if what Longshanks here says is right, then we'd better get out of town.'

Mahon was right but Gates always took his time about everything. Which fact gave some of the citizens of the town time to get over to the saloon to see what all the rumpus was about. Because they had no sheriff some of the tougher citizens, like the blacksmith and the owner of the general store, took it upon themselves to protect their own. Gates, Mahon and the others came face to face with them as they began to file out of the saloon. As they did so, it was not lost on the citizens of the town that here was a situation that was going to take some handling.

'What *have* we got here?' Gates called out in mocking tones as his eyes fell on the half a dozen or so gathered citizens of the town.

'We want to know who you are and what you think you're doing shooting-up the saloon like that?' the town's blacksmith, a giant of a Norwegian demanded to know.

'You do, do ya?' Gates replied, his voice full of contempt. His hand was already twitching to move in the direction of his gun.

Mahon, whose mind was still on the fact that Union soldiers were not far away, stepped forward and said, 'We're bushwhackers and only came into town to get some food and drink. Now there are Union soldiers riding this way and if you think you've got it bad with us, you's in for hell when they arrive. Best thing you can do is let us ride out of town and take them Union soldiers with us.'

'Either that or we kill you first and then kill the Union soldiers,' amended Gates.

Mahon could have wished that Gates would just shut up, but he had too much respect for his reputation. Even so, he couldn't see how acting like a bunch of outlaws and killing their own was going to help the Confederate cause, defeated or otherwise.

'Well, what's it going to be?' he asked of the gathered citizens.

'Get out of our town, then,' the

blacksmith said. 'And don't come back, ever.'

Mahon was ready to do just that, but Gates felt the blacksmith had the wrong attitude. They were heroes, had saved the skins of a thousand like him, and he felt they deserved better.

'Supposin' we just go and leave this town to the Union to sort out and bring to heel?' he said.

'Union's coming anyway. The war's over,' the owner of the general store replied.

'Over?' sneered Gates. 'Over? It's still just beginning.'

'Jonathon, I think we should be going. Longshanks here said they were only a few miles away. We can't make a stand here. It's not our way of doing things,' Mahon interrupted him.

Gates was momentarily in a dilemma. He could never walk away from a quarrel without leaving his adversary beaten. Since the war had started 'beaten' had meant dead. He heard Mahon but his eyes were fixed

40

on the citizens of the town standing in the middle of Main Street. 'Don't come back,' one of them had said. 'Don't come back.' The ingratitude of it had got to him and was gnawing at his innards. It continued to do so as he led his men to their horses and they all mounted.

'What about Lottie?' Mahon suddenly remembered.

'Leave her,' Gates said.

'We don't want any of you left here,' the owner of the general store said.

This was ingratitude gone too far. Whipping his horse around to face the store owner, Gates drew his gun and pointed it at him.

'Yeah, well if this town ain't big enough for you and her, one of you'd better quit it,' he muttered between gritted teeth. Then he slowly cocked his gun. A perverse satisfaction that he got from seeing the look of fear that filled the store owner's face made him pull the trigger. It also made him faster than the blacksmith, who had barely raised

41

the barrel of his shotgun before he was gunned down. Despite his better judgement, Mahon found himself helping to gun down the remaining citizens.

It was all over in a few minutes. The sound of gunfire had brought Lottie running out of the town's hotel to see what it was all about. She feared she'd see Union soldiers. Instead she saw Gates and the others reining in their shying horses. Seeing her on the steps of the hotel, Mahon grabbed the reins of her horse and pulled them free of the hitching rail and then hurriedly led her horse to her.

'Come on,' he said. 'We gotta get out of here. Union soldiers are comin'.'

Without hesitating she did as she was told and swung up on to her horse. 'What happened?' she asked.

'Guess,' was all he said in reply, as he spurred his horse into a gallop to join Gates and the others who were already eating up the length of Main Street as they rode out of town.

4

Gates and his men left Cave Hill a sorry town indeed. The war had raged all around it but somehow not over it. That is, until the arrival of Gates, and it had thought itself blessed. But no more. Five of its most prominent citizens were lying dead. Needlessly and pointlessly. As Gates and his men had ridden out of town, the rest of the citizenry slowly emerged from its buildings. In the forefront were the wives and other related womenfolk of the dead men and the low sound of choked-back sobbing filled the air. The undertaker and his assistant came out to attend, while other men collected in groups and talked about what had happened.

'This is what happens to a town that's without a sheriff,' remarked William D. Mortimer, the town's lawyer.

'I don't think a law enforcer would have made much difference here,' replied John Claude Bal, the town barber.

'Maybe not, but he'd be lying here dead now and not Henry, George, Mike, Herby and Dean, commented Mortimer. 'Which would have been the proper way of things. That's what you pay a sheriff for.' As he spoke Mortimer saw his wife rush over to where the storekeeper's wife was cradling her dead husband in her arms. 'We should have all come out,' he added.

'And all been killed,' said the barber.

A moment's silence engulfed the group while they all contemplated such a thought. Who then, they all wondered, would have taken care of the town's women and children? It was a thought that justified in each and every man's mind what could otherwise have been thought of as his cowardice. Excepting perhaps the lawyer's. He was a man of philosophy and the truth was not something his mind could easily mess with.

'Maybe, maybe not,' was his reply.

The undertaker and his assistant had begun to carry the bodies to their parlour when the Union soldiers mentioned by Longshanks came riding into town. Everyone stopped and turned to watch them. The sight of the Union blue of their uniforms brought no comfort to the citizens. These were the victors, even though they might be the ones to put an end to the excesses of the likes of the riff-raff who had just ridden out of town.

'What's been happening here?' Captain Hans Kung asked, as he reined in his horse near where the lawyer and the barber were standing.

I think we can guess, Gunter thought to himself, wondering if Gates could be behind it, or someone like him. The war was big and vast and his tiny offensive just a small part of it. He was worldly enough to know this.

The citizens were slow to answer. They perceived the Union soldiers mounted before them almost as aliens. Mortimer, being a lawyer, was forming the pragmatic approach but the fact that he was as a man more a Confederate than a lawyer still held sway in him. He couldn't be civil to their conquerors, but yet he knew they'd have to learn to get on with them if life was in any way to return to normal; if law and order were to be re-established across the South and crimes like that which had just happened were to be prevented.

'Bushwackers,' he answered.

'You sure?' Gunter asked.

'Sure I'm sure. I know the sort.'

'How many?' Kung asked, turning to glance at Gunter.

'Six, maybe seven,' he replied.

'Get any of their names?' Gunter asked.

'No.'

'What did their leader look like?'

Gunter's interest struck the citizens as more than academic.

'Well, we didn't get too close a look,'

the lawyer answered, 'but he was tall and dark with long black hair and was aged about thirty.'

'And he was mean, real mean-looking,' the barber added.

'Yeah, I know,' Gunter remarked, the sobbing of the newly widowed women-folk of Cave Hill registering with him suddenly and making his stomach turn.

'Which way they go?' Kung asked.

'They must have left a look-out posted up the trail. A rider came racing into town and they lit out of town that way,' the lawyer informed them.

'After shooting up the saloon and killing those town folks,' the barber added, pointing in the direction of where the dead men were being tended to by their widows and the undertaker.

'We going after them?' Gunter asked Kung.

Kung knew his men were hungry and thirsty and that their rations were low. Besides which it wasn't their method to pursue the enemy openly in a chase. They used guerrilla tactics, creeping up on him when he least expected it.

'No. They'll be miles away by now, Gunter, or be sitting lying in wait somewhere,' he replied, turning to face him. 'We'll rest up here for the night and leave just before dawn. It ain't often the men get to visit a town.'

It didn't please Gunter but he knew it was wise to defer to his friend Hans, who had not waited for the war to come to him but who had gone out and found it. Maybe, he thought, if he had done the same his family would be alive now. Still with the sick feeling in his stomach, he dismounted from his horse and tied it to a hitching rail as Captain Kung issued orders to his sergeant.

'And, Brown, I know I can count on you to make sure the men behave themselves. We pay for everything we eat and drink and anything we take away with us,' Hans added, as his sergeant went to pass on the orders to the men.

'Goes without saying, sir,' Sergeant Brown replied.

Looking on, the citizens of Cave Hill thought it all seemed rather civilized and they wished that their own people had conducted themselves in so disciplined a fashion. They showed how appreciative they were in the generous hospitality they showed the Union soldiers. It never really happened again in the years that followed the subjection of the South.

'Ain't there a sheriff or someone around here in charge?' Hans asked the lawyer and the barber who were still standing close by, not sure yet quite how to take the Union soldiers.

'Well, we ain't got a sheriff no more. At least he ain't been seen for some time now. And the town ain't big enough yet for a mayor. There's a kinda Chamber of Commerce that's been running things, exceptin' that half of 'em's dead now,' the lawyer answered.

'Well,' commented Hans, as long as y'all know the war's over now and the South lost it, everything should be all right after a while.'

Neither the lawyer Mortimer, nor the barber Bal replied. What the captain said had suddenly concentrated their minds and not left them with much to say.

'Well, we ain't here to occupy the town,' Hans continued after a second or two's pause. 'Our orders are to hunt down bushwhackers, so we'll be moving on before dawn tomorrow. But there'll be others following us. In the meantime, reckon I'll take myself a bath. What say you, Gunter? You joining me?'

He pointed his head towards the hotel. Gunter showed himself to be amenable to the idea and together the two men walked off in the direction of the hotel, nodding respectfully to the barber and the lawyer as they went.

'What d'you make of that?' Bal asked Mortimer when Gunter and Hans were safely out of earshot.

'I dunno,' replied Mortimer. 'We gotta wait and see, I suppose, if all the Union army behaves in so gentlemanly a fashion.'

'If they do, I'm gonna kinda get to wonderin' what all this war's been about,' said Bal.

'Yeah, well,' remarked the lawyer. 'I wouldn't go drawing any conclusions just yet. This peace has got a long way to go before it can safely be called just that.'

5

Gates hadn't known as he rode out of Cave Hill exactly who it was he was running away from, only that it was the Union army. He didn't fear the Union regulars, he just knew that there was a time and place to stand and fight them. And, as Jake Mahon had pointed out to him, Cave Hill was not it. He was camped now in a clump of trees some fifty miles west of the town and was mulling over the fact that the war was now over, at least the politicians' part of it, and he was wondering quite what future he should be mapping out for himself. The only conclusion he could reach was that he wasn't ready for any kind of peace. That he wanted to go on fighting. It was a way of life he'd come to like and he couldn't see himself turning back to farming. Had there been scope for him in the regular army, he might have enlisted, but it was obvious there wasn't going to be and he was left with little choice but to carry on as he'd done the previous four years. From a Confederate irregular though, he realized, it would turn him into an outlaw. A price, he thought, the new United States of America, whatever shape it chose to take, was going to have to pay for ruining the paradise that had existed in the South and which was now no more.

'Coffee, sir?'

It was Mahon. He and the rest of the men, along with Lottie, had been sitting around the campfire eating breakfast.

'You can drop the 'sir' now, Mahon,' Gates said to him, taking a tin mug of steaming coffee from him. The war's over. Call me Gates, Jon or whatever the hell you like. But not 'sir'.'

Mahon looked at Gates curiously, wondering what had brought such talk on.

'I thought we was gonna carry on as if it weren't and harry the Union army as much as we can.'

'Exceptin' in wartime, no one'll thank us for it. You saw what happened in town. The South's beaten. Anyone who takes on the army now will simply be an outlaw. It won't be Union generals hunting our hides, it'll be US marshals.'

Gates's way of thinking hadn't occurred to Mahon before and it got him thinking, mainly about Lottie. While he could see himself as any kind of enemy of the Union, he couldn't see Lottie as such and wondered what was to be done about her. He turned and looked to see her sitting brushing her lovely long hair by the campfire. Through all the hardships they'd endured she had retained her femininity. She'd never shirked from doing her bit in any of the skirmishes they'd got caught up in, but he couldn't see her becoming a common outlaw.

'Yeah,' remarked Gates, who'd seen Mahon become pensive and turn to look her way. 'She'll have to go.'

Mahon wasn't sure if he himself wanted to stay. Gates also sensed this fact.

'She wasn't involved in what happened at Cave Hill, but you were, Mahon. I'd say that kinda decides things for you, me and everyone, wouldn't you?'

Mahon had already made up his mind who was the villain of the piece in Cave Hill and resented Gates trying to lay some of the blame on him. Sure he'd opened fire on the citizens but not until they'd gone for their guns.

'That was you back there, sir,' he said. 'We could have left town and nothin' would have happened.'

'Well, we didn't and a lot of people got killed and you shot most of them, Mahon. Don't reckon what's left of the citizens of Cave Hill are gonna forget that.'

What Gates was implying was beginning to rile Mahon. It was a lie and there wasn't any justice in it. But he wasn't about to risk drawing on Gates, though his fingers twitched to. Instead, he simply strode back to where Lottie and the others were sitting around the campfire. Lottie could see he wasn't very happy and asked him what the matter was. When he told her she was equally indignant.

'Well, maybe we should just go our own ways, before we get any deeper into things,' she said. 'I never liked him anyway and only went along with things 'cause the rest of you did.'

They were overheard by the others, some of whom agreed with them. Those that didn't were as war-hardened as Gates and thought siding with him their best option. A return to pre-war occupations held no more attraction for them than it did for Gates.

Mahon thought for a moment and then declared, 'Well, if we're gonna split, we'd best do it now.'

Then he asked the others who amongst them was with him. Half a dozen showed their hands.

'Right,' he said, 'best I go tell Gates.'

Gates had sensed that Mahon was not happy and kept an eye on him as he walked back to the campfire. He was too far away to be able to hear what was said but guessed.

'You quittin' then, are ya?' he said to Mahon when he returned.

'War's over, Gates, and there ain't nothin' but the end of a rope to be gained from pretending otherwise.'

Gates was sitting with his back against a tree, sipping at the coffee Mahon had brought him. He didn't answer Mahon at first. He looked as mean as he had standing on the plankwalk outside the saloon in Cave Hill.

'How many you taking with you?' he asked at last.

'As many as want to come. Maybe half a dozen. But I ain't taking any with me. If they want to quit it's up to them. I'm going home, to see what's left of it. I'm needed there now. There ain't nothing left for us to do out here no more.'

Gates felt the anger of being walked out on rise in him and felt inclined to go for his gun and blow Mahon all the way back to from where he'd come, but for once in his life he considered what it would gain him. He knew Mahon to be fast and himself to be at a disadvantage sitting as he was on the ground beneath him. And there were the others. Those that chose to join him. A woman was present and there was no telling what they'd do to show off to her. Best, he thought, to let him go. They weren't worth shit anyway, if a scrap of paper drawn up between politicians could mean so much to them.

'Well,' he said, drinking the last of the coffee and slowly getting to his feet, 'if that's how you feel, don't suppose there's much I can say to alter things.'

Mahon was on his guard against Gates suddenly trying to tough it out. The man had a reputation, after all.

'But you leave the girl,' Gates

suddenly declared, showing the kind of mean streak that earned him his devil's tag.

'What d'you say?' asked an angrily incredulous Mahon.

'I said, the girl stays,' repeated Gates.

Mahon thought for a moment, first looking over at Lottie and then back at Gates.

'And what makes you think you have any say in who stays and who goes? The war is over, and that is that.'

'I said,' repeated Gates, 'the girl stays.'

Mahon realized that he was wasting his time trying to talk any kind of sense to Gates and decided he'd just collect his things and ride out of the camp, with Lottie and whoever else wanted to go with him or who just wanted to leave.

'You're not listening, Mahon, are you?' Gates spat at his back. 'I'll say it one more time, the girl stays.'

Mahon knew the kind of situation he was in. He was young but the war had made him mature fast and he was now as hard as the hardest. Gates had barely uttered the last word when with lightning speed Mahon turned and drew his gun.

'I heard,' he said, cocking it. 'Seems, though, you didn't hear me when I asked what made you think you had the right to give orders to anyone any more?'

Reflecting on what Mahon had said, Gates regretted that none of the men standing around were his men yet, that they'd not had time to become so. He'd made assumptions about Mahon and he'd been wrong. Well, he thought, he could let him go this time and make him pay later.

'OK, farm boy,' he said. 'Best you go home, then.'

He and Mahon eyeballed one another for a moment and then he turned and sat down again with his back against the tree. He was going to wait and see who was left behind when Mahon, the girl and whoever else rode out of camp.

Mahon though did not lower his gun. Keeping it pointed at Gates, he took a few steps backwards and said to Lottie and anyone else who wanted to leave to collect their things and saddle up. Collecting his own things and calling on Lottie to saddle up his horse for him, he kept his gun at the ready. Gates for his part didn't take his eyes off him, keeping his mouth all the while locked in a sardonic sneer.

Six men left with Mahon and Lottie, leaving seven behind to throw in their lot with Gates. Mahon was the last to ride out of camp and he didn't holster his gun until he was safely out of harm's way. Those that had stayed behind simply stood about waiting to see what Gates would do next.

★   ★   ★

By the time Mahon and the others rode out of camp Captain Hans Kung and his men had been on the trail a couple of hours. Scouts had been sent ahead to look for any sign of Gates. One of them came back with news of a sighting of a group of men on horseback.

'They look like bushwhackers to you?' Kung asked the man, who had plenty of experience of identifying the kind of wild-looking men who made up the roaming packs of bushwhacking Confederate irregulars.

'I'd say so. There were about ten of them riding fast, heading west.'

'Could be them, Gunter remarked. 'What we gonna do, Hans?'

'Go get 'em,' Hans did not hesitate to reply.

'How we gonna know for sure it's them?' Gunter asked. He was anxious to make Gates pay, but he wasn't interested in making just anyone do so. The sight of yet more innocent dead in Cave Hill had reinforced that feeling in him.

'We'll know,' replied Hans. 'Believe me, Gunter, we will just know. Right, Brown,' he continued, speaking to his sergeant, 'we'll split up and come at them from the north and south. You take half the company and go south and we'll come at them from the north.'

Both Captain Kung and his sergeant knew the terrain they were in well. They had ridden all over the state in pursuit of Confederate irregulars. They were heading into a slightly hilly country dotted with small spinneys and coppices of trees that would provide them with plenty of cover. There were farms here and there but not many and in this area hardly any. Sergeant Brown also knew the strategy Kung intended to use. He, Brown, would get close to the enemy but not too close and he would wait for his officer to make the first assault. In this case it would be a pursuit until either the bushwhackers took cover in a woodland or else turned and fought them head on. Either way once the firing started Brown would be in there providing a deadly crossfire.

'How far away do you say they were?' Kung asked the scout.

'By now five miles, maybe six,' the man replied.

'Right,' said Kung, looking at Brown, 'let's up and at 'em. Gunter, you're with me.'

From past experience, the rest of the men knew whom they were to follow. Although the day was getting hot and the going was sweaty all except Gunter were beginning to feel the adrenalin rise. He was feeling a tight knot deep in the pit of his stomach. Except for the resistance he and his family had put up to Gates's attack on them at the farm, he'd never taken part in any kind of pitched battle before. As he rode at the side of hardened soldiers, not knowing what to expect, his heart was beating furiously. His mind, filled with the picture of Gates standing looking down at the womenfolk of his family, whom he'd just slaughtered, was whirling. It wasn't long before the band of bushwhackers came into sight.

On first seeing them from high land, Captain Kung reined in his horse and got out a telescope. Pulling it out to its full length, he put it to his right eye. He counted seven horsemen dressed in the kind of gear bushwhackers were known to wear riding steadily in the shape of an arrowhead. It was obvious they had no idea they were being watched, let alone pursued. Extending his fields of vision all round the bushwhackers he could see no sign of Sergeant Brown.

'Looks to me like it's them,' he remarked, passing the telescope to Gunter.

Wiping sweat from his eye, Gunter put the telescope to it and twisted it until it focused on the band of horsemen. None of the features of the riders was clear enough for him to be able to distinguish them but the general appearance of them all had a familiar look about it and he was prepared to believe that their leader could be Gates. One of them seemed to have particularly long, flowing hair, but then, this was nothing unusual in these mixed-up times.

'It could be,' he said to his friend Hans.

'Time to find out,' was his reply.

He took the telescope from Gunter and cast his eye about again in search of Sergeant Brown and his men. He was about to give up looking, when he caught sight of a group of men on horseback riding out from the cover of a large wooded area north of the band of bushwhackers. Pleased, he pushed the telescope into itself and, putting it back in its case, said, 'Brown's there. Let's go.'

They set off at a gallop. There were small clumps of trees to ride around and in and out of as they raced towards their quarry. All were armed with Remington New Model Army revolvers and took their lead from Captain Kung as to when to draw them. He gave that lead at less than five hundred yards. At two hundred yards he fired his first shot, the signal that invited Brown to join in.

'What the — ?' exclaimed Mahon, as

he saw the man to his left take a hit.

He soon caught sight of both Brown and his men coming at them from the north and Kung and his from the south. Union soldiers, he knew immediately. The man to his left had managed to stay in his saddle after taking the first hit, but Mahon saw him now take a bullet in the face and fall from his horse. His first thoughts were for Lottie. He knew she could fire a gun, knew that she could fight as well as any man, but his natural chivalry made him want to keep her from all harm. Lead was flying all around them and another of his men fell from his saddle. Thankfully, he could see Lottie was still in hers.

Casting an eye about for somewhere to take cover, he saw immediately ahead of them a thick clump of trees and decided to head for it.

'Over there,' he called over his shoulder, reining his horse to take his men in a straight line to it. They were still a few hundred yards distant from

Kung and Brown.

So far all the casualties had been on their side and as they rode into the cover of the trees, leaping off their horses before they had stopped, another of their men took a fatal hit. Mahon grabbed Lottie and pulled her to the ground behind the large trunk of a deciduous tree. From either side of it they both emptied the barrels of their Le Mat revolvers. Two of Brown's men and one of Kung's fell before they were able to ride around the clump of trees that Mahon had lead his men into and take up positions around them.

'There's too many of them,' Mahon said to Lottie.

The Union soldiers and the bushwhackers were only yards away from one another and Gunter could see the faces of their adversaries very clearly. He saw that none of them was Gates and that one of them looked awfully like a woman. This latter fact shocked him and he turned his gunfire away from the tree that she and Mahon were hiding behind. Knowing that Hans was under cover not far from him he felt that he ought to call out to him that they were attacking the wrong people. But equally he supposed that if they were bushwhackers, and no doubt they were, otherwise why were they putting up a resistance, they had probably killed many of his own race, most of whom were Unionist sympathizers.

More men fell on both sides and soon of the bushwhackers only Mahon and Lottie were alive. Mahon decided if he were to save Lottie they would have to give up. He said as much to her.

'I don't want to die,' she said to him. 'Besides which, ain't this war over?'

'They know we're irregulars and there are many like Gates who ain't given up yet and who won't. And the Union must know it,' Mahon replied, ducking down from a bullet that had struck the tree an inch from his head. 'Hold your fire!' he called out to his attackers over the din of the gunfire. 'We're surrendering!'

Captain Kung heard him but it took him a number of seconds to get his men to put up their weapons. There was usually little mercy shown to bushwhackers, so savage and non-discriminating had been the many atrocities they'd committed against the civilian population as well as the Union armies, and the Union soldiers were already getting ready in their minds to witness a good hanging.

'All right,' Captain Kung called out to Mahon and Lottie, 'throw away your arms and stand up with your hands in the air.'

Mahon knew he could expect no mercy but he hoped they'd show some to Lottie.

'It's a woman with me,' he called out to the men surrounding him, infuriating Lottie. She'd fought for months now alongside men and hadn't then and didn't now want or expect to fare differently from them. Mahon asking for it made her want to jump up and go out in a blaze of glory.

'What did you want to go and say that for?' she asked of Mahon, who gave no reply, thinking the answer must be obvious.

Despite being taken aback by Mahon's declaration, Kung was not prepared to soften his stance.

'I said throw away your arms and stand up with your hands in the air,' he repeated in authoritative tones.

Without making any reference to Lottie, and in such a way that the Union soldiers could clearly see he'd done so, Mahon threw his Le Mat away and got to his feet. He expected Lottie to do the same, which she did, though with a show of obvious reluctance.

'Right,' said Captain Kung. 'Now step forward with your hands in the air.'

It was not until Lottie did so that it became unmistakably apparent to the Union soldiers looking on at what were obviously female curves that what confronted them was indeed a woman. While nothing surprises war-hardened men, Gunter was a novice and he felt

71

welling up inside him the natural protectiveness towards her that all men in normal society feel for a woman when she is at her most vulnerable. His eyes became fixed on her and were only momentarily caused to turn away when Hans asked him if Mahon was Gates.

'No,' he replied absentmindedly, 'that ain't him.'

6

Gates was not a happy man. The war was over, the Confederacy had lost and now it was in a state of disarray. Union soldiers were beginning to show up in the area in numbers and the highways and byways were beginning to stream with refugees and soldiers returning home. The economy of the old south was in tatters and a man, being no longer able to live on the spoils of war, was going to have to start helping himself to whatever little remained to be shared amongst the civilian population. And not just that; Union ropes were stretching the necks of any irregulars they caught. He was going to have to keep one step ahead of the game, if he was to make sure his wasn't one of them.

So he robbed stores, shot, wounded and murdered where he had to and then availed himself of the hospitality of friendly homesteaders, all the while steering clear of Union soldiers. And he was never happier than when he was tormenting German immigrants. This meant that while he remained elusive, Captain Hans Kung and Gunter were kept informed of his continuing presence in the locality. As they went about enforcing the peace and consolidating the occupation, they kept an eye out for him, knowing their paths would inevitably cross.

But in the thick of all this and when logic says they should not have done, Gunter and Lottie fell in love.

'She ain't had nothing to do with any of this,' Mahon gallantly declared, as he stepped out defenceless from the tree behind which he and Lottie had taken cover.

'Have you been held prisoner by this band?' Hans asked.

'No, sir,' Lottie began to say, only to be interrupted by Mahon declaring that she had.

By this time Gunter's heart had already gone out to her, imagining that she had been taken in a raid like the one the womenfolk of his family had all been killed in.

'Mahon, shut up,' Lottie turned round and snapped. 'I wasn't taken prisoner by no one. My husband was killed and I decided I was gonna avenge his death by killing as many of you Yankees as dared cross the Mason-Dixon line.'

'Now that ain't true and you know it, Lottie.' Mahon insisted.

''Tis so,' insisted Lottie, turning to Captain Kung and pointing at Mahon. 'Now if you're gonna hang him, you gotta hang me, too. Why, I've probably killed more of you darned Yankees than him, anyways.'

Mahon was stunned to see Lottie turning herself into a southern belle, while Gunter and Kung couldn't help but be inwardly amused. They didn't want to have to hang her and were quite prepared to let Mahon give the lie to her protestations of having participated in bushwhacking ill-deeds. They could save her neck but Mahon's was a different matter. Union soldiers had just died, chasing what were, now that the war was over, nothing less than common outlaws, whatever they liked to call themselves before. If they didn't stretch his neck, they'd be sending the wrong message to the populace at large and those higher up would be asking why, especially if he went on to commit more crimes.

'Someone get a rope,' Kung suddenly ordered.

'No,' Lottie gasped, turning and making a grab for her discarded Le Mat pistol.

As she did so the guns of all the Union soldiers in Captain Kung's patrol were pointed at her and cocked. She was not to be deterred though and was only saved by Gunter running forward and grabbing her. Mahon knew better than to make any kind of move.

'Get your hands off me,' snarled

Lottie as Gunter held her tight in a bear-grip, trying to restrain her.

'Aw, Lottie, shut up!' barked Mahon, 'and let these Yankees get on with what they must do.'

'Where's that rope?' Kung asked, keeping an eye firmly focused on Mahon.

Sergeant Brown suddenly appeared at his side with one.

'Throw it up over that branch,' Kung ordered him, 'and bring a horse up.'

'You can't, Lottie insisted in begging tones. 'We're prisoners of war and deserve to be treated as such.'

'The war's over, Miss, and besides, the people you killed back in Cave Hill were civilians, not soldiers and that amounts to murder.'

'That was not our doing, that was Gates,' argued Lottie, still being held in a bear-hug by Gunter, though she was no longer struggling to break free. 'That's why we split up from him. The war was over and we was going home. We didn't want no part of what Gates was doing.'

'Is that so?' Kung asked Mahon.

'Yeah,' replied Mahon, though with little conviction. He had by now resigned himself to being hanged. He had done terrible things in the war, to both Union soldiers and civilian sympathizers, whether proven to be so or not, and was quite willing now to pay for it.

Lottie had become limp in Gunter's arms and he slowly let them fall from around her. Whatever Hans decided to do with Mahon, he knew he'd lay down his own life before he'd let anything happen to this woman. He'd been helpless to stop Gates slaughtering the womenfolk of his family and if only to right the wrong of that he had to stop a woman being summarily executed now. It seemed to him logical that it should be the way his war ended.

Sergeant Brown had thrown the rope over the branch and had made a noose of one end of it. As he tugged on it to test its effectiveness a private brought up a horse and placed it under the rope.

'Get him up on it,' Kung instructed Brown.

Brown did as he was told. Mahon put up no resistance as his hands were tied behind him and the noose put over his head. Nor when he was thrown up on the horse. Lottie, though, began to protest again and made a another grab for her pistol.

'I wouldn't,' Kung said to her, 'we can shoot you as easily as hang you.'

Gunter was appalled to hear these words addressed to a woman.

'Hans,' he appealed to his friend, 'there must be some other way. She's already told you they had nothing to do with the killings at Cave Hill.'

Captain Kung knew he had to do what was expected of him by his men, if only to save face, his own and that of the army. But yet she was a woman. And if he spared her life, then he had to spare Mahon's, too. He looked into Mahon's face. He didn't see the face of evil, as he might have done if he'd been looking into Gates's. He saw a man who had no doubt simply done what the times had demanded of him. Sergeant Brown could see the dilemma his captain was in and decided he had to help him out.

'Sir, we could take them to the camp at Mud River and they could be tried there.'

Brown's suggestion only slightly eased Captain Kung's situation. The Union army despised bushwhackers and he had his orders. Seconds, which seemed like minutes to everyone watching, passed while he struggled with his thoughts. He tried to avert his eyes from those of his friend but he could see life again in them, the kind of life that had not been there when their paths had crossed and he told him of the slaughter of his family. He knew what had brought that life back. He knew a man smitten when he saw one. His friend was decent and good. Was this woman? Was the man on the horse with a noose around his neck?

'We could do that sir,' Brown said again.

'All right,' said Captain Kung at last. 'But if they try to escape, they are to be shot.'

'Thank you, Hans,' Gunter said.

'Tie her up, Gunter,' was his friend's reply. 'Brown, detail two men to watch them.'

Later when Gunter and Hans were alone Gunter again thanked him.

'I only hope,' answered Hans, 'that the military tribunal doesn't find them to have been part of Gates's company of bushwhackers at the time he murdered your family.'

These words concentrated Gunter's mind somewhat, but they did not quieten his heart.

'The man said they had taken her prisoner,' he reminded his friend.

'If that turns out to be the case, all well and good, Gunter. But if it doesn't she's a heartless, murdering bitch, who if she didn't directly have a hand in killing your family, no doubt had a hand in killing others.'

Captain Kung and his men had made camp to eat and Gunter looked over to where he could see Lottie and Mahon sitting tied back to back against a tree. It had been love at first sight, he knew this, and could not believe that life could, after all he had been through, deal him so cruel a blow as to put her out of his reach and for such tortuous reasons.

'Then we'll find Gates and we'll ask him,' he suddenly declared. 'And if she has had a hand in killing anyone, then I'll put the noose around her neck and hang her myself.'

7

All round the old South rumours flew of hoards of gold and valuables stashed by the rich and powerful at the beginning of the Civil War. Many of those treasure-troves, it was known, were used to keep the war going during the Confederacy's darkest days, but there were some that had remained hidden. Gates got to hear of one that had purportedly been brought up from Tennessee by rich plantation-owners and hidden with poor relatives who farmed in Quality Valley.

'It is still there, not ten miles from here,' said Bill Morrison, a chancer who'd drunk most of his life away, even through the darkest days of the war.

'What makes you say that?' asked Gates.

While Gates's men were keeping a look-out on watch, they were in the drinking and eating area of a ramshackle store built on a crossroads in about the middle of the county. The store was the only building then on the crossroads. Union soldiers and refugees were crowding the roads and the storekeeper was doing great trade with those of them that had any money or worthwhile barter. Gates had bought a bottle of whiskey with a yankee silver two-dollar bit, which for some time had been the preferred currency in the southern states.

'Well, I ain't heard anybody say it ain't,' was Morrison's reply.

Gates knew the man of old and had often received titbits of useful information from him as he'd traversed this part of West Kentucky seeking out Union sympathizers. But the man was a drunk and some of his stories had seemed a little far-fetched, if true in essence.

'You sure it weren't just a few pieces of family silver and some gold chains?' he asked him. 'Any money they brought up will be worthless now.'

'I'm telling you, Gates, there was gold and silver a-plenty and a big hole was dug and all of it was put in it. It was the talk of Quality Valley for miles around,' Morrison insisted, pushing his empty shot glass forward for Gates to fill it up.

'Are the owners of the farm still there?'

'The old folk and women still are. The men and boys all went off to fight the Yankees.'

'They German?' Gates asked.

'Na,' replied Morrison, getting out some makings and building himself a cigarette. 'They was Scottish or something but they've been here awhile.'

He offered Gates his makings. Gates took them, indicating with a nod of his head that Morrison could help himself to another drink. Building himself a smoke, he thought for a while about what Morrison had told him and then asked, 'Reckon you could take me to this farm?'

'Sure could,' replied Morrison. 'If you cut me in.'

Gates didn't reply, but simply gave Morrison another drink, which, like all the others, he first took a sip of and then knocked back in one go. Then he said, 'I ain't ever been a greedy man, Bill, and I ain't ever been niggardly returning favours. You'll get your cut. That's if there's anything there to have a cut of.'

Gates had had a drink or two more himself and was finishing a smoke, when one of his men came in to tell him there was a company of Union soldiers approaching the crossroads.

'How many?' Gates asked him.

'Twenty, maybe more,' the man replied.

'Right then, Bill,' Gates said, getting up from where he'd been sitting and letting his hands wander to the security of his guns. 'Best we be making tracks to Quality Valley, don't you think?'

'Yeah,' was all Morrison said in reply, his eyes falling on Gates's bottle of whiskey, which was only half drunk. 'We ain't leaving that, though, are we?'

'Don't be silly,' Gates answered, picking the bottle up and recorking it. 'Here, you take care of it,' he added, handing the bottle over. 'And we'll finish it later.'

He stepped out on to the veranda of the shop in time to see the Union soldiers ride by. He eyed the captain of the troop and was eyed back in turn. Fearless defiance had always been his way and he'd learnt to reckon on most people leaving him well alone. The captain thought there was something untoward about the men he saw spread out around the old store but equally he knew he and his men were somewhat exposed. If they went for their guns, they'd probably mostly all die. So he rode on, clocking what he saw. He'd pull up somewhere down the road to take stock.

Gates did not take his eyes off the soldiers until the last man rode past them. Gold and silver were on his mind now, not making any kind of stand against Yankees.

'Right,' he said to his men, as the Union troop rode away from the crossroads. 'We got us some work to do.'

None of them knew what he was talking about, but they swung up on to their horses and followed him and Morrison as they headed off the road and across country. They'd covered about five miles of wooded countryside when dusk began to fall.

'How much further do you reckon?' Gates asked Morrison.

'Ten, maybe fifteen miles,' Morrison replied.

There was no moon and Gates could see that within about fifteen minutes it would be dark, and before long it would be pitch dark. It was too far to try and reach the place where Morrison reckoned the stash was hid. He knew of a few friendly farms in the vicinity but decided he'd not avail himself of their owners' hospitality this night. No one would like him for what he planned to do and he reckoned it best not to advertise his presence in the neighbourhood. The war was over and people's attitude to things was beginning to alter somewhat.

'OK,' he said. 'We'll ride on 'til it gets dark and then make camp for the night.'

'You're the boss,' was Morrison's reply.

★　★　★

The captain of the troop of Union soldiers that had ridden past the store at the crossroads had pulled up his men a few miles down the road. He'd thought on the matter and had decided that under cover of dark he'd lead his troop back to the crossroads and, if it looked as if the men he'd seen loitering about were still there, he'd stake it out until morning and then challenge them. If they'd gone, he'd find out from the storekeeper who they were and where they'd gone. He had no doubt the men he'd seen were the gang of bushwhackers he'd been told were causing trouble in the county but he was equally mindful of the fact that they were dangerous and accomplished fighters. Ambush was the only way of being certain of destroying them.

In daylight he and his men had to ride around the endless stream of people on the move, but at night the way was clear, with everyone pulling off the road to eat and bed down. It was obvious to him when they got back to the crossroads that the suspected bushwhackers had gone. Nevertheless, he told his men to spread out and lie low and he and his sergeant rode up to the store and dismounted. There was obviously some drinking going on inside but otherwise things were quiet. They became quieter still as he and his sergeant opened the door and walked in. The store had been something of a hangout, not just for bushwhackers and other irregulars, but for all manner of opportunists throughout the war. The sudden appearance of Yankee soldiers in their midst gave the gathered company something of a surprise. The captain was under no illusions that he had to keep the upper hand by demonstrating the conqueror's command of the situation. While his sergeant remained on guard and vigilant by the door, he strode up to the counter and addressed a man whom he took to be the proprietor.

'Those men that were here this afternoon, can you tell me where they have gone?'

'Men? Why hundreds have passed by here today. How am I supposed to know where they were heading? Reckon most of them was heading home somewhere's.'

'You know who I'm talking about. Now, am I gonna have to order this place to be burned to the ground or are you gonna tell me?' the captain snarled uncompromisingly.

The eyes of the men gathered in the

store looked from one to the other and then to the captain and the sergeant. The storekeeper looked beyond the captain to some of his more regular customers and then back.

'I told you,' he said, 'I don't know who in particular you're talking about.'

'Well, then, let me put it to you straight. I have reason to believe there were bushwhackers here today and that they must be known to you. Now you can tell me where they've gone or am I gonna have to burn the place down?'

'Look, captain, I have sat out this war for the last four years, taking nobody's side but just hoping it'd leave me alone to go about my business. You ain't telling me now that the war is over that I'm gonna become a casualty of it? 'Cause if you are, that ain't fair.'

Becoming impatient with the man's bluffing, the captain turned and began to walk out of the store, ordering his sergeant as he went to round up a few of the men and set the store on fire.

'All right, all right, all right,' the

storekeeper suddenly declared. 'They rode off east across country. But I don't know where they was going or what they were intending to do. They just came and they went, like they've done all through the war.'

The captain stopped and turned back to face the storekeeper.

'And you helped keep them supplied?' he said.

'Like he told you,' a man sitting at a table volunteered. 'He was just taking care of business. Ain't no one can blame a man for that.'

'Guess you could say that's what the Union was doing,' the captain, turning to face him, replied. Then turning to his sergeant he repeated the order he had previously given. 'This place is surrounded,' he announced to the gathered company, 'and when I give the order you'd all better come out with your hands up. Anyone tries anything they'll be shot.'

Then he turned and followed by his sergeant he walked out of the store.

'Call them out, Sergeant, and burn it. It'll be a lesson to people for miles around.'

The store burned through most of the night, causing the utmost consternation to the storekeeper, his family and patrons, while becoming a spectacle for people on the move who had camped nearby for the night. As its ashes smouldered in the dawn hours of the next day, fifty miles away due west Captain Kung and his men were striking camp in readiness to continue their sweep across West Kentucky as they made their way to Fort Quality near Mud River. They'd still not picked up any new intelligence on Gates and were beginning to wonder if he'd gone West.

'A lot of his sort are doing that,' Hans remarked to his friend.

'I don't think Jonathon Gates is,' replied Gunter.

'What makes you say that?'

'I don't know. He considers this part of the world to be his domain. His kind are like the princes of old. The war gave him a false sense of his own strength. When he came to our place he came like someone whose right it was to crush anyone he felt he had a right to, as if someone or something had given him power over all. He will not feel so sure of himself anywhere new. Anywhere that will call into question his supremacy.'

The conviction with which his friend had spoken made Hans think on for a moment or two without saying anything. When he did not speak Gunter continued, 'We Germans had a view of our own about the South and its slavery. We supported the Union and in the South it was the wrong thing to do and look how we have suffered. I have lost my whole family. You lost your father, Hans. And now that the war is over it turns out we were on the right side. Gates was on the wrong. He will not rest until he has made us pay the price for that. I did not fight in the war but now that peace has come here I am fighting alongside you, seeking to avenge the slaughter of my family.'

Again Hans could find nothing to say in reply. He had seen the change that had come over his friend since he set eyes on Lottie. His friend was a good man; could it be now that having found love he had lost the need to seek revenge for the death of his family? Could it be that his friend wanted to go West, to get as far away as possible from a world that had seemed like the promised land, but which the war, as it had been fought by men like Gates, had shown to be no different from any other inhabited by mankind?

'You are a civilian, Gunter. You do not have to be fighting. You could go now and leave Gates to me.'

'And what about the woman, Hans?' Gunter asked.

'Maybe,' replied Hans, 'it is better you do not find out if she is guilty or not.'

Gunter now was the one whose thinking-on robbed his tongue of an answer. Lottie had taken no real interest in him since leaving the place where she and Mahon had been taken prisoner. But still something deep in his heart made him want her. Could he really bear it if she turned out to be as much a devil as Gates?

'No,' he said at last. 'I have to know.'

He looked over to a stream where Lottie was washing the sleep out of her eyes. Hans's eyes followed Gunter's. He was glad Gunter had been there, because if he hadn't that woman would have been hanged. And a woman was a woman; he'd never harmed a hair of one before and was glad of it. Mahon was still sitting tied to a tree, finishing a plate of pork and beans. Hans's eyes went to him. He didn't know how he felt about him. If he'd ridden with Gates, then he deserved to die. He, Hans, had dispatched to their maker many men in this war. And what was a man? Well, certainly not the soft, sweet creature a woman was.

'Come on, Gunter,' he said after a

few minutes' more meditation. His tone of voice was suddenly hard, reflecting perhaps the fact that he had suddenly remembered he was indeed a soldier with a job to do. 'Let's go find Gates and bring this matter to some kind of resolution.'

Sixty miles west Gates was himself striking camp and getting ready to ride.

8

'How far are we from there now?' Gates asked Morrison as they prepared to swing on to their mounts.

'Six, maybe seven miles,' was Morrison's reply.

'OK,' Gates said. 'Now you gotta tell me something about these folk. You say they ain't got any menfolk with them.'

'Nor any young-uns, unless, of course, they survived the war and are back already, but I doubt that. There's an old-timer or two. That's all.'

'In that case it should be easy. By the way, what's their name?'

'McKenzie.'

There were eight men with Gates and Morrison. They didn't need to be given any instructions. They were a murderous crew by nature and would simply follow any lead Gates showed them. If he drew his gun, they'd draw theirs. If

99

he started firing, they'd start firing at whatever he was firing at until Gates stopped. Morrison had slight qualms about what they were about to do, but alcohol was his master and he'd do whatever bought him more of it. The night before, after everyone had bedded down for the night, he'd drunk the last of the bottle they'd bought from the store at the crossroads and his palate was already craving a taste of what he didn't have.

They passed by a number of farms as they ate up the last few miles. They gave a wide berth to them, not wanting to draw anyone's attention. But of course everyone knew they were there, if not exactly to what ends. Gates's reputation preceded him wherever he went and people felt it wiser to keep out of his way than to pry into what he was doing in their neighbourhood.

They pulled up in a spinney a few hundred yards from the McKenzie homestead. From the look of it, it was obvious that it had once been a profitable concern. The war hadn't bothered it that much and it was still a lovely timber-built house with a flower-garden and well-kept barns. So much so that Gates couldn't help but feel that some of the hoard of silver and gold belonging to the McKenzies' relatives had already been spent.

'We'll hold off for a bit,' he said to his men, 'see how the land lies.'

As he spoke a little girl of about ten or eleven came out of the house and down the steps of the veranda. She headed for the flower-garden, singing and talking to a doll as she went. The only one of Gates's gang touched by the sight was Morrison. He had three daughters of his own but his wife had long since taken them and gone back to her family in Georgia. She had not been able to take his drinking. He hadn't seen his little girls since his wife had left with them and he had often wondered how they had fared through the war. He guessed he'd never know but hoped someday he would.

Gates watched the house and the yard for another half-hour or more before deciding there were no men around who might have been a threat. He'd seen an old-timer come out and take the girl off to what looked like a vegetable-patch but that was all. A beautiful woman had come out and hung some washing on the line and he and his men had admired her, wondering who, if not all of them, would later get to possess her. The scene was an idyllic one and would have remained so now that the War Between the States was over, but for Gates's evil intentions.

'Reckon it's time we said hello,' he said to Morrison and the others, spurring his horse into a walk that took them to the front of the house.

'Whoever's in there come on out,' he called out to the folk inside.

Molly McKenzie, who was indoors shelling some peas into a pot, suddenly turned with a startled look to her elderly father. Putting the peas and the pot aside, she got up from the chair she was sitting in to see who it was calling them out. She had not recognized the voice. Her father went to get up and follow her.

'Stay there, Father,' she said. 'I shall only be a minute.'

Peering through the window in the door before she opened it she was made uneasy by what she saw. Such men, she thought to herself, rarely brought less than trouble. Stepping out on to the veranda, she pushed her hair out of her face and fixed it in place with hairgrips that were already there.

'Good morning to you, ma'am,' Gates greeted her as she came through the door. 'I was wondering if you'd have some refreshment for my men and me. We've ridden a long way trying to avoid Yankee soldiers.'

Molly Mckenzie realized she had no choice but to answer yes — southern hospitality demanded it — but she wasn't happy about it and wished her husband and other of the menfolk who had gone off to fight were there.

'If you and your men will make yourselves at home on the veranda,' she said to Gates, 'I'll bring you out some lemonade.'

'Why, that's mighty neighbourly of you, ma'am,' Gates replied, his ingratiating tone of voice and manner unconvincing.

Molly turned and went back into the house.

'Who are they?' her father asked. He was elderly but not yet feeble.

'I don't know, but I don't like it,' Molly replied.

She was always mindful that any strangers who suddenly showed up at the farm might have heard of her family's hidden wealth but she knew it was well hidden and could not easily be found. What contributed more to her unease about Gates and his men was the way they looked. Dressed in martial gear, with long unkempt hair and wrapped around with cartridge-belts and gun-holsters, they had the look of what they were, bushwhackers turned desperadoes.

'I don't like the look of them, Father,' Molly said. 'Best you stay in here and watch the children. Where is Annie?'

'She was in the flower-garden last time I saw her,' he replied.

He didn't like the threat Gates and his men represented and he wished his sons were there to confront them. He had always been a game old boy but of late he'd been short of breath and unsteady on his feet.

'Perhaps I should go out the back and fetch her in,' he suggested.

He remembered the shotgun he always kept loaded and ready for use in the barn and reckoned, while pretending to go for his granddaughter, he could instead go into the barn the back way and fetch it. Then he'd go up into the loft where there was a little window that would give him a good view of the house and a straight line of fire.

'All right,' his daughter said. 'But be watchful. It's getting near lunchtime. If you see the others coming back from the fields, warn them to stay away. I don't want those degenerates out there getting any ideas about Cathy and Rachael.'

What she said worried the old-timer and he became all the more determined to go and get his shotgun and be ready. As Molly prepared something for Gates and his men to drink, he went out the back. Annie was nowhere to be seen in the flower-garden and he supposed she had wandered towards the fields to watch for the others coming back, something she did most days when they were out there working. Taking one last lingering look, he turned and began to walk towards the back of the barns. A few minutes later Molly carried a tray of lemonade and her precious few glasses out to Gates and his men.

'Got anything stronger?' Morrison asked her as she put the tray down on a table. Gates was rocking backwards and forwards on a swinging chair and the others were variously sitting or leaning up against the veranda posts and railings.

Mary was quite taken aback by Morrison's request. Seeing this and scowling at Morrison, Gates said, 'Don't pay him no mind, ma'am. He ain't ever been taught any manners.'

Morrison said no more about hard drink and gulped down a glass of lemonade. Gates and the others followed suit. Then Gates said, 'Nice place you got here, ma'am. Seems the war passed it by. You living here alone?'

'No,' replied Molly, lying, 'my husband's in the fields along with his brother and some helpers.'

'Is that so?' Gates mused, knowing from what Morrison had told him she was lying.

Molly made no reply. It was gone midday and the day was already getting hot. An insect was buzzing about her face and she flicked it away with her hand.

'I heard differently,' Gates continued. He'd emptied his glass and was now looking at the day through it in what Molly thought was a menacing kind of way. She wondered if he had indeed heard about her relatives' stash and had come looking for it. 'I heard other things, too, ma'am. Like you and your family have been holding out against the Confederacy things that everybody else gave up to keep the armies armed and supplied against the Yankees.'

Molly knew instantly she had guessed right.

'We gave up everything we had whenever it was asked for,' she declared.

By now her father was in place with his shotgun trained on the men on the veranda. He was sweating and finding it hard to keep his hands from shaking. He was mopping his brow as Gates began to tell Molly that he knew of the gold and silver and that he'd come on behalf of the Confederacy to collect it.

'I'm sure I don't know what you're talking about,' she said bluntly, beginning to collect up the glasses Gates and his men had emptied. 'We gave up our menfolk, wasn't that enough?'

'I thought you said they were in the fields,' Gates replied, suddenly getting up and barring Molly's way back into the house.

Molly was fumbling for a reply when a shot rang out and a windowpane shattered. The shock of it made her drop the tray of glasses. Before they had hit the ground Gates and his men had simultaneously drawn their guns and spun round to see where the shot had come from. To a man they realized it could only have come from one place, the direction of the barns. No sooner had they come to this realization than another shot rang out and one of the men fell to the floor of the veranda with half his head blown away.

'Inside,' Gates ordered, pushing Molly ahead of him as he dived in through the front door. Within seconds his men, having fired back, were inside with him, taking cover behind windows, the glass of which they smashed out with their guns.

'Annie! Father!' Molly gasped to herself, as she suddenly realized the shots could only be coming from one person.

'Who is that firing?' Gates demanded of her in vicious tones.

Molly didn't answer at first, too frightened and too confused to know how to reply for the best.

'I said who's that firing?' Gates asked again, this time rushing up to Molly and grabbing her by the hair, pulling her head back and shoving his gun into her face.

'My father,' she replied. 'Don't fire back. My daughter is there with him.'

On hearing what she had to say, Gates angrily threw her back against a wall and strode to the centre of the room, thinking fast.

'Frank, Dick,' he ordered two of his men, 'go round the back and take him by surprise. Kill him if you have to. And anyone else who's with him.'

'No!' Molly screamed, collecting

herself and before anyone could stop her running out of the back door.

'God damn it!' Gates snapped. 'Get her and bring her back. Alive. We need her to tell us where the gold and silver is hid. The rest of you fire on the barn and don't stop until I tell you.'

As the firing started, Molly's father let go another shot, which penetrated the timber of the house and whistled past Gates's head. Seconds later Frank and Dick came bursting through the back door, returning with a struggling Molly whom they threw heavily down on to the floor.

'Right, bitch!' Gates snapped at her. 'This time you're going out of the front door.'

Just then another shot from her father's shotgun whistled through the air, this time finding a home in Dick's left shoulder. He reeled and fell to the spot on the floor where he'd earlier thrown Molly. Seeing this, Gates grabbed Molly by the arm and marched her to the front door.

'Keep up your fire,' he ordered his men, as he opened the door and, using Molly as a shield, began to edge out on to the veranda.

Molly's father had been about to let go another shot, when he saw his daughter being pushed out of the front door. Holding his fire, his hands began to shake more than ever. He'd taken a risk shooting before, because of the danger of hitting Molly by mistake; this time he knew he dared not shoot at all. It was what Gates had counted on.

'Hold your fire, men, he instructed. Then he called out to Molly's father, 'listen, you stupid old man, one more shot from you and your daughter dies. Are you hearing me? Now throw down your rifle and come out with your hands up. You got ten seconds and then I'm gonna kill her.'

The old man was suddenly filled with panic. He knew Gates's type and knew he meant what he said. Except, as he had guessed by now, he knew he had also come for his brother's gold and silver. Well, Molly's life was worth more than any amount of treasure and he decided he had to throw out his shotgun.

'All right,' he called back to Gates. 'Only let my daughter go. Let her walk away. I know what you've come for but you won't get it if you hurt my daughter.'

That's better, Gates thought. Then he called out, 'All right, but throw out your weapon first.'

The old man pondered this, not knowing if he could trust Gates, who'd already shown himself beneath contempt by using a woman so at all. Yet he knew he didn't have any choice. He wished again that his son was there to protect them all.

'So, what's it gonna be?' Gates called out to him after a few seconds of getting no reply.

Without replying in words, the old man threw his gun out from the loft window.

'There,' Gates said, pushing Molly

into the swinging chair and calling out to Morrison to go get the gun. Another two he ordered to go get the old man and bring him to him.

As he and Molly waited, Annie and a young aunt suddenly appeared running up to the house. They stopped in their tracks when they saw Gates with gun drawn and Molly sitting in the swing chair looking put upon.

'We heard gunfire,' Rachael, her younger sister said between trying to catch her breath. 'What's happening, Molly? Who is this man?'

While she was speaking Annie leapt up the steps to the veranda and threw herself into her mother's arms.

'It's all right,' Molly said in soothing tones, while offering a furrowed brow and shaking her head in such a way to her sister as to tell her not to pry. 'Mummy's OK. There's nothing for you to worry about.'

Little Annie wasn't convinced but she didn't ask any more questions. She'd seen enough men coming and going throughout the war and knew when best to leave things to the adults to sort out. Nevertheless she clung to her mother as if she'd never let go. Rachael simply stood and watched.

'Come up here, you,' Gates ordered her.

She did as she was told and was directed to sit down in one of the chairs on the veranda and say nothing. Just then one of the rougher-looking elements of Gates's gang came out of the house on to the veranda, casting a leering eye at the pretty Rachael as he did so.

'Go get the old man,' Gates ordered him, tilting his head in the direction of the barn.

'There's no need,' a voice suddenly said. It was Jim, Molly's father, coming striding out shakily from the big barn. 'I'm coming.'

★　★　★

The gunfire heard by Rachael and Annie had been heard by someone else.

115

Captain Reynolds and his troop, the Union soldiers who'd burned down the store at the crossroads. They'd been following the trail of Gates and his men and it had brought them to within a mile of the McKenzie spread. While not knowing the McKenzie spread was there, they easily ascertained from which direction the gunfire was coming and set their horses galloping towards it.

Meanwhile Gates was being confronted by Molly's father, who was being anything but compliant.

'Now where is it?' Gates demanded of him, meaning their relatives' gold and silver hoard.

'You'll know just as soon as you let my family go,' Jim answered him.

'What d'you mean, let your family go, you stupid old man?'

'I mean get your men out of my house and let my family go in there. Then I will talk to you alone out here.'

Gates looked at him and then at Molly. Annie was still clinging to her mother. Then he cast his eye upon Rachael. What a pretty young thing she was! He was not the raping sort. More his thoughts were running along the lines that he should have done with it and kill them all, one by one until the old man told him where the treasure was hidden.

'Look, old man, I'm gonna ask you one more time and if you don't give me the answer I'm looking for you won't have a family to worry your grey-haired old head about. Now do I make myself clear?'

'I don't think I'm making myself clear, Mister whoever you may be. You kill one of us you kill us all. Now I'm the only one who knows where that gold and silver is hid. You harm a hair on the head of anyone of my family and you ain't ever gonna find it, whether you dig up every last inch of Kentucky.'

Morrison, though a drunk, was basically a good man. He thought they'd arrive at the McKenzie's, take the gold and silver and ride out again.

'Let the women go inside,' he suddenly said to Gates. 'There ain't nothing to be gained from terrorising the whole family.'

Gates, who was a ruthless autocrat, resented Morrison's interference and told him to shut up. But Morrison, to whom the McKenzies personally were not unknown, was finding it hard to resist the feeling that things had gone far enough. He asked Gates what harm it could do to let the women and Annie go inside.

Gates had suddenly had enough. Feeling every muscle in his body tense, particularly those that controlled his trigger-finger, he did as his mean streak ordered him to do and shot Morrison dead. As the women screamed. Gates thought it would make clear to the old man just who was running the show. His arrogance, though, was to be his undoing, for the shot that punched into Morrison's heart told Captain Reynolds, who was less than a few hundred yards away, exactly where Gates was.

'Now,' Gates snarled at Jim, pointing his gun at Rachael, 'you gonna tell me where the gold and silver is or am I gonna have to start killing your family one by one until you do?'

Jim, who, realized that Gates was going to have it all his own way and that he was just going to have to hope he wouldn't harm his family, reckoned he now had no choice but to tell him what he wanted to know.

'OK, come with me,' he said, 'and I'll show you where it is.'

But 'Nobody move!' a voice boomed from the woodland surrounding the McKenzie's homestead. Gates looked around him, not exactly in utter surprise, since he was an outlaw and used to being jumped suddenly, but more like an animal poised to spring into attack in his own defence.

'Lay down your arms and no one'll get hurt,' Captain Reynolds continued. 'We are Union soldiers and you are surrounded on all sides.'

The whole McKenzie family breathed

a sigh of relief. Could their ordeal be at an end? But Gates had no intention of laying down his arms or giving up what he now thought of as his hostages.

'Don't do anything,' he instructed those of his men who were still in the house. 'Stay where you are. If they open fire shoot back.'

Captain Reynolds, from his experience in dealing with Confederate irregulars, quickly realized a gun-battle was going to ensue whatever. His concern, though, was for the McKenzie family and how best to keep them out of the line of fire.

'All right,' he said, 'Let the family go and we'll give you a head start.'

'Why should I trust you?' Gates called back.

'Because, I'd say, you ain't got much choice. Now lay down your arms and let the family go.'

'You can have the family, but my men stay in the house and we keep our arms,' Gates called back.

'All right,' replied Reynolds, 'but

don't try anything.'

Gates grabbed the old man by the arm and using him as a shield walked backwards to the house.

'Dick,' he said, 'Get the women and the girl on their feet and line 'em up at the top of the steps.' Dick did as he was told. 'Right. Now get the horses and take them round the back and wait for me and the others.'

Captain Reynolds and his men looked on apprehensively, sensing that Gates was planning to try and make an escape before the family was out of the firing line.

'Right now,' Gates called out. 'My men are gonna be waiting in the house. You open fire and the family's all dead.'

'I told you,' Reynolds called back. 'Let the family go and we'll give you a head start.'

Gates didn't reply but simply smirked to himself. He didn't give a damn about the family, it was the gold and silver that were on his mind.

'Now then,' he said in hushed tones

to Jim. 'You gonna tell me where that hoard of your relatives' is or am I gonna order my men to open fire on the soldiers?'

'It's buried about fifteen foot down in the top right-hand corner of the big barn,' Jim was very pleased to be able to tell him, knowing there was no way he'd have the ability to dig up it up without running the risk of having to share it with the soldiers. A smirk spread across his face.

Gates realized at last that he was beat but he wasn't going down without a fight. 'OK, old man,' he said. 'You win this time, but I'm taking this lady here with me. Now I know you ain't fool enough to want to share what's hidden with the Union, so I'll be back. If that gold ain't still there when I do get back you're all gonna die. Get me?'

The old man nodded in reply, looking over at his daughter, a sinking feeling in his stomach. It wasn't over yet and they weren't out of danger.

'OK,' Gates said to Dick, indicating

Molly. 'Take her and get going. Quietly. Go east to Turner's Holler and I'll meet you there.'

When Captain Reynolds saw what was happening he guessed what Gates was up to but still felt he didn't want to risk any of the family getting shot. Still, he thought, Gates wasn't going to have it all his own way. He instructed two of his best men to make their way round to the back of the house and told them to open fire on the gang when they tried to make their getaway but to be sure not to hit the woman.

'I told you to let the family go,' he called out to Gates. 'You've had plenty of time and my patience is beginning to run out.'

'You can have 'em now,' Gates called back, turning and striding into the house. 'Get going and fire into the air and don't stop until we're clear away from here. I'll cover your backs,' he instructed his gang.

The sudden burst of gunfire made Rachael, Annie and Jim jump with fright. 'Come on,' Jim said to his daughter and niece, 'follow me,' and he began to run down the steps towards the woods in the direction Captain Reynold's voice had come from. Reynolds saw them coming and thought it best to let them reach him safely before doing anything about Gates.

The sound of gunfire was suddenly mixed with cries of pain as the two soldiers Reynolds had sent to the back of the house began to pick off Gates's men when they came through the back door. They were crack marksmen and made every shot count. It was terrifying for Molly, as the man gripping her arm fell and his blood splattered her, but the skill and rapidity with which the Union soldiers shot meant she was unhurt.

As his men died, Gates managed to avoid getting hit. Being the last to leave the house, he had time enough to realize his men were being picked off one by one. Looking back to the front of the house, he saw the McKenzies making their escape. He would have shot at them but to shoot women and old men in the back as they tried to get away was something too far beyond the pale, even for him. Instead, his mind turned to saving his own skin. His mind was a whirr of rotten, selfish ideas on how to achieve this, the last of which took him diving out of the back door of the house to grab Molly. She had been standing about in a daze, expecting any moment to die.

'Right, bitch,' he snarled as he grabbed her by the hair from behind. 'Do as I say or you're dead.'

The two Union soldiers were taken completely by surprise but anyway dared not shoot at Gates for fear of hitting Molly.

'Shoot, and she's dead,' Gates called out, as if to reinforce their fears.

Molly didn't struggle but fell almost in a faint into his arms. He looked around for a horse and saw one nibbling at grass on the edge of the woods. He recognized it as Dick's. He cast an eye about looking for his own mount but it was nowhere to be seen; he decided Dick's horse was better than none. Keeping a sharp eye on where he knew the soldiers were and keeping Molly in front of him as a shield, he edged his way backwards towards it. His mind was still thinking rapidly. Should he take the woman or cast her aside when he was safely out of danger? She could be his passport to the hoard of gold and silver but would she also slow down his escape and keep the army hot on his heels? She was still in a faint and was now dead weight in his arms. Still keeping her in front as a shield he managed with difficulty to climb into the saddle. As he did so Captain Reynolds with his men came running into the woods at the back of the house.

'Goddamnit!' Gates swore when he saw what was happening. He was glad that he hadn't tried to take the rest of the family with him.

Seeing Reynolds appear, Gates decided he had no choice but to keep Molly hostage.

'Don't anybody try anything,' he called out loud, as he took hold of the reins of the horse and got ready to ride off. 'Or she's gonna be worse than dead.'

Watching him disappear into the woods, one of the Union soldiers had him squarely in his sights, but as the horse rose up and fell so too did Molly slip in and out of those same sights.

9

'Looks like someone's burnt down the crossroads store,' Gunter remarked to Captain Kung.

They were still riding the trail to Mud River and were coming up to the crossroads.

'More'n likely some drunk knocked over an oil lamp,' Hans laughed back in reply, remembering how the crossroads store was one of the places his and every young man's parents had warned their sons to stay away from for fear of their being led astray.

'Well, whatever happened they made a very good job of it,' Gunter laughed. 'Pity, though, we could have had ourselves some good ham 'n' eggs for breakfast this morning.'

It was just gone nine in the morning. Summer was well on the way and in Kentucky people liked to get going early before the day got too hot. The war had not changed that fact. Captain Kung and his men had long since had breakfast but it was the usual dry and salted fare and something fresh would have gone down very well. They pulled up beside the ashes of what had been the crossroads store.

'What happened here?' Kung asked a man who seemed to be hanging out there.

'Soldiers burnt the place down a few nights ago,' the man spat out bitterly.

'Union or Confederate?' Gunter asked.

'Your kind,' the man replied, 'Reckoning we was harbouring bushwhackers.'

On hearing the word bushwhackers Captain Kung sat up in his saddle and looked around him.

'You the storekeeper?' he asked.

'Was,' the man replied, 'and will be again as soon as the timber arrives. I survived the war and it's gonna take more than you Yankees from up North to put me out of business.'

'Which way they go from here?' Kung asked him.

The storekeeper still felt an allegiance to the bushwhackers but had come to realize since his store was burnt down that the South had lost the war and that there wasn't any point any more in resisting the march of progress. This was how he and many like him were now beginning to see the success of the anti-slavery movement in the form of President Lincoln's war. Without the least attempt to mislead or deceive, he raised an arm and pointed east, saying, 'In that direction. Rumour has it they had a spat with bushwhackers at the McKenzie homestead and that their leader got away, taking one of the womenfolk hostage.'

What he said brought Gunter up fast. 'What did you say?' he demanded of the storekeeper.

Lottie and Mahon, both of whom's hands remained tied and who were closely guarded, heard the conversation and had a pretty good idea just who the bushwhackers the storekeeper was referring to were. They looked at each other but said nothing.

'I said . . . ' began the storekeeper in reply to Gunter's question. He'd barely finished when Gunter said to his friend Hans, that it had to be Gates. 'I never did think he'd go West to Texas,' he added.

Lottie had noticed how Gunter had looked at her and she had realized that he harboured romantic feelings towards her. To her he was not an unattractive man and she had been flattered by his attentions. Added to which, she was war-weary and found the idea of settling down with someone to start again to live some sort of civilized life an appealing prospect. Besides which, of course, he had played the major part in saving her neck so far. It might be that all there was between her and the scaffold was Gunter and his determination to bring Gates to book. And she, too, had come to hate Gates. That was something they both had in common and to see his downfall would be something that would bond them. She listened now intently as Gunter extracted all the information he could from the storekeeper and then turned to Captain Kung and said, 'We gotta go after him, Hans.'

His friend knew his thoughts were no more just of revenge, but of clearing Lottie's name too.

'I know,' his friend agreed. He took the reins of his horse and ordered his troop to move out. They were heading east.

★   ★   ★

Jonathon Gates thought he had lost the Union soldiers. Shortly after escaping into the woods he had let Molly go, with the words that he would be back later to collect the gold and silver. He had simply let her slip from his grip and then spurred his horse into a gallop away from the scene. She was found an hour or so later wandering in a daze by a group of soldiers which Reynolds had split from his company along with others to form search-parties. Shots were fired in the air as a prearranged signal to let Reynolds know that Molly had been found and the soldiers returned with Molly to the McKenzie homestead. Reynolds decided that he and his men should stay on for a few days to bury the dead and help the family come to terms with what had happened to them. They were there still when Captain Kung, Gunter and his men rode on to the homestead to check out what they'd been told at the crossroads. Molly, who had, as needs must, made a quick recovery, was sitting in the swing chair watching Reynolds and Kung make one another's acquaintance, when she saw a face she thought she recognized. Lottie, though she was still dressed in men's clothes, was no longer disguising herself as a man. Her long, thick, beautiful hair hung over her shoulders. Molly knew that hair could belong to nobody else and got up from the swing chair to go greet her old friend, whom she'd known since they were little girls at Sunday school.

'Why, Charlotte Jones, is that you or do my eyes deceive me?'

Lottie had known whose homestead they were riding to but had chosen for her own reasons to say nothing. Now as Molly recognized and greeted her she was unsure as to how to react.

'It is you!' Molly exclaimed as she drew close to her. 'Don't you know me? I'm Molly Ford as was till I married?'

Both Reynolds and Kung turned to see what was happening. Lottie still said nothing but looked rather embarrassed to be seen by Molly with her hands tied and in her present circumstances.

'Don't you know me, Lottie?' Molly continued. 'And why are your hands tied? What has happened? What is this all about?'

Lottie still gave no reply. Seeing that some sort of answer was required, Gunter answered for her. 'She's under arrest, ma'am, for involvement in bushwhacking and outlaw activities.'

'I ain't denying the bushwhacking,' Lottie suddenly said, 'but I am denying that I'm an outlaw.'

Molly, still exhausted from what had happened before, found it hard to take in what was being said about her old school-friend and simply stood back aghast. Charlotte Jones had come from one of the best families in the county and Molly could not believe that she and the dishevelled, trail-hardened person she was looking at were one and the same person.

Collecting her thoughts and suddenly pulling herself up straight, she demanded that Lottie be untied and allowed to come into the house with her to take some refreshment. Captain Kung stepped forward and repeated that Lottie was under arrest and would have to remain so.

'She could,' suggested Gunter, 'be asked to give her word that she will not try and escape.'

Captain Kung considered the matter for a moment and then asked Lottie if she would agree to give such an undertaking. Before answering Lottie looked at Mahon. 'Go on, Lottie,' Mahon said. 'The war's over and we've got to look to our own futures now.'

'All right,' Lottie agreed.

'Good,' Captain Kung declared, ordering Sergeant Brown to untie her hands.

Lottie got down from her horse and Molly led her into the house. As she went she turned to took at Gunter who smiled back at her affectionately. 'Thank you,' she mouthed to him. He simply nodded back, his heart swelling with a love for her that grew by the day. As Lottie and Molly disappeared into the house, Captain Kung turned to Captain Reynolds and declared they'd better talk about how they were going to track down Gates.

10

After letting Molly go Gates headed for Turner's Holler. He rode through thick woodland as familiar to him as the back of his hand but which he knew the Yankees would not know their way through. That was if they did give chase, which somehow, in his experience, he doubted they would. He'd been lucky to get away with his life, though men like him seldom considered such matters with much seriousness. After all he had been getting away with his life all through the war and it had gained him the reputation of being invincible. He wasn't fool enough to believe in such nonsense, but nevertheless he didn't consider too deeply whether in this life he was meant to live or die; he just went on, at first fighting the rebel cause, and now fighting his own. In the latter cause, even as he fled the scene of overwhelming odds, he couldn't get the thought of the gold and silver lying buried in the McKenzies' barn out of his mind. He was sure he'd find men in Turner's Holler who'd be interested to know of its existence.

At Turner's Holler, a makeshift camp for irregulars and bushwhackers, made up largely of sod huts, there was a lot of confusion and uncertainty at what was happening in what had become their traditional stomping grounds since the end of the war. People who were used to being masters of their own world were suddenly finding their world shrinking. The Union armies of occupation were suddenly proliferating through the old South and Kentucky. All the other men inhabiting the camp had stories similar to Gates's to tell. Except none of them told of a treasure not taken by the Confederacy in the war. Because so much wealth had been grabbed by the Confederacy no one found it easy to believe that the treasure spoken of by Gates did in fact exist.

'Well, I'm telling you it's there,' he insisted, 'and I almost got my hands on it.'

'Supposin' them Union soldiers have got their hands on it by now. And besides, you ain't even told us yet where it is.'

This was said by one of the veterans of the irregulars' struggle against the North.

'And no more am I going to,' replied Gates, 'until I know who's with me in going back for it and who ain't.'

'Well, if you can't prove it's still there I don't see any point in going looking for it,' the veteran said, reiterating his point. 'Most of the men have already started West and I reckon that's the best any of us can do. There ain't nothing left for any of us here now except trouble. Them Yankees done won the war and they's gonna be calling the shots around here now.'

'Well, I ain't leaving Kentucky

empty-handed and anyone that wants to come with me can come now,' Gates declared.

Along with the others he was sitting in a large turf dugout. Summer was almost on them and the air was beginning to get hot and full of insects. Most of the men stank and they all wore clothes that looked as if they had seen better days. And indeed they had, for they all came from families that had lived good lives on farms and cotton- and tobacco-plantations before the war. Their lives had been changed for ever and none of them would ever again be able to live a settled, domesticated sort of life. Especially not the tough life of sacrifice that was going to be needed to rebuild the war-ravaged economy of the South.

'All right,' one of the men said. 'I'm with you, Gates.'

'Me, too,' echoed a number of others.

All in all a dozen men threw in their lot with Gates. His reputation for survival preceded him and the men, all born camp-followers who would not have known how to survive on their own, needed someone to follow. He himself threw a look of quiet satisfaction at the veteran.

'Well, good luck to you,' the man said. 'You're gonna need it.'

'Luck don't come into it,' was Gates's reply. But he wasn't about to get into any philosophical discussion about it. 'We'll leave first thing in the morning,' he said to his new men. 'Make sure your weapons are in good working order. And don't come if'n you ain't got enough ammunition to take on a company of Union soldiers.'

Some of the men who had volunteered to go with Gates had Sharps breech-loading rifles. Gates looked on with pleasure as they began to clean them. If the Union soldiers were still at McKenzie's homestead when he got back there, it was his intention to surround the place and attack them before they knew what had hit them. It was, however, his belief that the soldiers would have moved on by then. Empty-handed. No Southerner would believe a Yankee suddenly to be his friend, even if he had just saved his life, and he did not see the McKenzies voluntarily handing over to the Union soldiers their hoard of gold and silver. They might have dug it up and hidden it somewhere else to prevent him from laying his hands on it but that was about all he reckoned he'd come up against in going back. His new company of men were merely insurance against that not being the case.

★   ★   ★

In fact both companies of Union soldiers had left the McKenzies's place. Molly had told Captain Reynolds that she'd heard Gates telling one of his men to take her to Turner's Holler and she'd told him exactly what Turner's Holler was.

'Well, I think it's time Turner's Holler was cleansed of its vermin,' he'd declared, turning to Captain Kung. 'And come to think of it, Captain Kung, I cannot see why you have burdened yourself with two known bushwhackers, when the usual procedure is to have them shot.'

Night was drawing in and they were sitting on the veranda drinking coffee and Gunter was with them. Gripped by a sudden feeling of panic, he looked to see what his friend Hans's reaction was going be to what Reynolds had said.

'That was the accepted policy while war raged but now that it's over I don't see what's to be gained by continuing it. And besides, as you can see, one of them's a woman whom the other maintains was press-ganged into bushwhacking. That being the case I reckoned it was better to take them to Fort Quality for the matter to be decided there by someone higher up the ladder than me.'

'The war might be officially over but I don't see men like Gates accepting the fact,' Captain Reynolds replied. 'And as long as they don't they'll keep firing on us. Therefore, when they're taken prisoner it's best they're shot or hanged.'

'Women, too?' Gunter asked.

As he spoke, Lottie appeared from inside the house. Molly had insisted she change into a dress and had given her one of her best to wear. Looking at her, none of them could imagine her body hanging from a rope or lying riddled with a firing squad's bullets.

'Very nice, ma'am, very nice indeed,' remarked Captain Reynolds, 'but we're planning to ride out of here at first light. Best you change back into your bushwhacking clothes by then.'

Like many German immigrants, Gunter's sympathies had lain with the North and their determination to ban slavery, but he nevertheless was quite ready to view Lottie as a hero of the Civil War. He respected Hans but he began to wonder what he was doing helping him to take Lottie into a Union stronghold. He couldn't have cared a damn about what happened to Mahon but he suddenly began to feel that he should try and help Lottie escape. Especially given the attitude of Captain Reynolds, which he thought was probably representative of most of the Union forces that were now beginning to occupy the South. Falling in love had softened him somewhat, but not so much that he did not still want to take his revenge against Gates for slaughtering his family. If he helped Lottie escape he might never see her again, yet if he didn't who knows what fate might befall her? Unless he went with her.

'Maybe I should take your prisoners to Fort Quality while you continue to track down Gates. They can only be a burden to you,' Reynolds suggested to Hans.

Hans was mindful of his friend's position but equally felt his duty as a soldier came first and quickly decided that Captain Reynolds was right. Besides, he thought, Gunter could, if he preferred, go with them to Fort Quality, or he could remain with him and his company of men and help track down Gates. The choice was his. And if he could not get the woman out of his mind, he could go to Fort Quality later and look for her once Gates had been found and dealt with. He felt though that he needed to talk to Gunter alone about it. On the pretext of needing to make sure his men knew they'd be leaving early the next morning, he left the veranda, instructing Gunter to go with him. He told Captain Reynolds that he'd give consideration to what he'd suggested and that he'd talk to him further on the matter before he bedded down for the night.

Gunter would not hear of Lottie being taken out of his friend's hands. Hans tried to reassure him that she'd receive a fair hearing at Fort Quality but Gunter insisted there was no guarantee she'd get there. Without saying anything to his friend, he decided he'd escape with her that night and that he'd find her a hiding place with friends in Butler county where his farm was.

'I lost my whole family. Gates murdered my mother and my wife, my sisters and my brothers' wives. I could not bear to see another woman harmed. If Lottie goes with Reynolds, then I will have to go with her. I owe that much at least to the women of my family.' He was lying about going with Lottie but he did not want to make his friend's position any more difficult than it was. Nor could he tell him of his plans to escape with Lottie that night. 'If I go with Lottie, once I know she is safe I will return to help you find Gates, that's if you haven't done so already.'

Hans didn't try to change his friend's mind. He could see that it was made up.

'All right,' he said. 'I'll tell Reynolds I'm sending you as her escort.'

There was no moon but even in the darkness of the early evening the relief on his friend's face was visible. 'And don't worry about Gates,' he added. 'I will find him.'

'I know you will,' Gunter said to him. 'I know you will.'

As Hans turned to walk back to the house to talk to Captain Reynolds, Gunter began to plan how in the night he would help Lottie escape. His biggest problem was going to be letting Lottie know of his plans. All the soldiers were to be bedded down in the barns, with two men on picket duty all night. Molly offered to let Lottie sleep in the house, an offer Lottie was only too pleased to take up. Captain Reynolds objected to it at first but on receiving a reassurance from Lottie that she would not try and escape in the night, he finally agreed to it.

'Good,' said Molly. 'That's settled then. You can have Annie's room at the back of the house and she can sleep with me.'

'There will of course be a guard placed outside the house all night,' Captain Reynolds said as he stood up and got ready to leave the veranda to go to his quarters in the big barn.

'Good,' said Molly. 'Should that brute of a man decide to come back he will get a surprise.'

'Why?' asked Reynolds. 'Are you expecting him to return.'

Molly thought quickly. Of course Gates had said he would return for the gold and silver but she had said nothing of its existence to the Union soldiers and did not want them finding out about it now.

'Well,' she said, 'he came in the first place, didn't he?'

'Yes, ma'am, but I don't think you need to worry about him coming back while we're here. He's probably a hundred miles away from here by now, anyway.'

Gunter felt like remarking that they shouldn't count on it but he said nothing for fear of making Captain Reynolds increase the guard. Instead he said good-night to every one and walked off to a small barn in which he had been billeted. He was relieved to think, firstly, that Lottie was not going to be sleeping with Molly, and, secondly, that there was indeed going to be just the one guard. He felt that as a problem that guard could one way or another be fairly easily dealt with.

It didn't take long for the soldiers and the McKenzie family to settle down for the night. Gunter slept with all his clothes on and was ready to move the moment he felt it safe to do so. Hans was sleeping in the barn with him but far enough away not to be disturbed by any noise he might have made as he threw back his heavy ground sheet and got to his feet. Hans did in fact stir in his sleep as Gunter began to leave the barn but he was a heavy sleeper and had not heard or sensed anything.

Gunter crept to the barn door and looked out to see where the guards were. The only one he could see was by the house leaning up against the veranda railings. He looked to Gunter to be dozing off. Relieved, he crept round to the back of the house and looked up at the windows. There were three of them. One he supposed to be on the landing, those either side of it to be bedrooms. But in which bedroom was Lottie sleeping? Since he was going to have to go into the bedrooms to investigate, he decided it was best to go in through the landing window and enter the bedrooms through the doors.

He found an easy way up to the landing window and was just about to try and prise it open when he heard the guard coming round from the front of the house. He had climbed on to a small slanting roof and reckoned that if he flattened himself against it as much as he was able and kept still he would not be seen. The roof, though, was at a steep angle and it was all he could do to stop himself slipping down it. Holding on to a narrow windowsill, he watched the guard walk by underneath. The roof suddenly creaked and the guard stopped to look up but in the dark saw nothing. After a few seconds he continued on his rounds, disappearing around the side of the house.

Gunter waited some moments to make sure the guard did not suddenly come back, then he attempted to open the sash-cord window. Luckily it gave quite easily and he was able to climb in through it. He wished there had been a full moon, for it seemed very dark and he had a job to make out where the bedroom doors were. The floor-boards creaked as he walked over them and he felt sure that someone in the household must be awoken by the sound of them. He hoped, if anyone did awaken, it would be Lottie.

His eyes became better accustomed to the dark and as he felt his way carefully along the walls of the landing he came upon what was obviously a door. It moved slightly inwards as he touched it and he was relieved to think it had not been firmly pushed to. Opening it wide enough to be able to slip through, he crept into the room. It seemed to him there were two people in the bed and he guessed he must be in Molly's room, since she had said Annie could sleep with her. Quietly he withdrew from the room, gently pulling the door to behind him. He retraced his footsteps along the landing wall until he found another door. This one was firmly closed and he had to apply a firm grip to the door-handle to get it open. It creaked and made a clicking noise as it opened. Gunter paused for a moment and when he was sure it had not woken anyone, he gently pushed the door open and crept in. There appeared to be just one body in the bed and Gunter guessed it had to be Lottie.

Putting his hand firmly but gently over her mouth he whispered her name into her ear, 'It's me, Gunter. Don't worry, Lottie, it's only me.' She woke immediately.

It was obvious she was not going to struggle or scream out and so he removed his hand from her mouth.

'What is it?' she asked, sitting up on her elbows. 'What do you want?'

'You've got to escape, Lottie, and I'm coming with you. Otherwise anything could happen to you once we reach Fort Quality.'

Knowing that he was with the Union soldiers, Lottie at first wondered why he should care but then remembered exactly why. He was in love with her. 'All right,' she said. 'Wait outside while I get dressed.'

Gunter waited on the landing for what seemed like an age, until at last Lottie, dressed in the clothes she had worn as a bushwhacker, appeared at his side.

'Right,' he said, 'I came in through the window but I reckon we should leave by the back door.'

'But there's a guard down there,' Lottie warned him. 'I can climb through the window.'

'No, it's too risky. The roof is not very strong and felt as if it was going to give way under me. Come downstairs with me and I'll take care of the guard. He'll probably be in the front sleeping anyway,' Gunter said.

The stair-treads creaked noisily as they went down them but still no one appeared to be wakened. Gunter led Lottie to the back door, which opened easily, but as they stepped out on to the back porch the guard suddenly appeared from round the side of the building. He was as startled to see them as Lottie and Gunter were to see him. But Gunter was a hunting man and he reacted quickly to the sudden appearance of what to him now was quarry. Before the guard could lift his rifle he was on top of him. Lottie heard a gurgling sound and in the next instance found herself being led away from the scene by Gunter, who she noticed, wiped clean the blade of a knife before slipping it into a scabbard on his left side.

Gunter took her to where he knew

the horses were. Lottie was as able to saddle a horse as he was and a few minutes later they both led their chosen mounts into the woods. Before long they were riding away from the McKenzie spread.

11

When it was discovered the next morning that Lottie had escaped and that Gunter must have helped her, Captain Kung was dismayed but somehow understood. Captain Reynolds, however, felt it vindicated the Union stance, saying that no one in the South could be trusted, adding that, woman or no woman, Lottie should have been hanged when she was first taken prisoner. He was minded, he spat out when the dead guard was found, to hang Mahon there and then.

'I don't think he can be blamed for this,' Captain Kung said in his defence.

'He's a rebel, ain't he?' Reynolds insisted.

'He's a prisoner of war and it would be murder to hang him without going before a properly convened military tribunal.'

'Tell that to that man's family,' Reynolds remarked, pointing at the dead guard.

Captain Kung didn't answer, but instead ordered Sergeant Brown to get together a burial detail to bury the dead guard.

'And make sure your prisoner is part of it,' Reynolds ordered.

Captain Kung nodded at Brown, indicating that he was to obey the captain. Then turning to Reynolds, he said, 'After the men have had some breakfast we'll go look for them and if we find them I'll arrest them both and bring them to Fort Quality.'

Reynolds simply sneered knowingly. 'Gunter's a friend of yours, ain't he?' he said.

'He is,' replied Kung, 'but he wasn't any friend of the Confederacy. None of we Germans were. And don't forget bushwhackers killed his whole family. He was riding with us to hunt down Gates and he won't be happy until he sees him pay.'

'Then what's he doing helping one of them escape?'

'He fell in love, I suppose. She was as much a victim of the war as he was. Our side killed all her family. Surely we should look upon their falling in love as a miracle, a sign that God has not deserted us altogether.'

Reynolds sneered. 'And the guard? How does he fit into the miracle?'

Captain Kung could find no reply to make.

'Or are you gonna say 'God works in mysterious ways'?' Reynolds continued.

'I don't presume to understand any of it,' Hans replied. 'We won the war, but if we're to win the peace, we're all gonna have to take a long look inside of ourselves and try to get on as Americans.'

With that he turned and walked to where his men had been billeted. He was met by Sergeant Brown leading a small contingent of men, in the middle of which was Mahon, to bury the guard. 'Look sharp,' he said to him.

'And when you've done that get the men ready to move out.'

'Yes, sir,' the sergeant replied smartly.

'And then hand the prisoner over to Captain Reynolds.'

Mahon suddenly looked afraid. 'Don't worry,' Captain Kung said to him, 'you'll get a fair trial.'

'Sir.'

★　★　★

Gunter had in fact decided to take Lottie and lodge her safely with friends. Lottie wasn't keen but she realized the long adventure was over and that she had to return to some sort of ordinary domestic life. What he hadn't told her was that he was then going to leave immediately and finish searching for Gates. He had not liked having to kill the guard and reckoned it was the only thing he could do to make amends for it. Falling for Lottie had turned his world upside down and confused the main purpose of his life, which had been to avenge the murder of his family. Killing the guard had brought this one thing back into focus. It was all Gates's fault, even the killing of the guard, and he had to still pay for it. While he remained at large in the county, he had to pay for it.

★   ★   ★

Gates and his men rode out of Turner's Holler on a trail that would have them on the McKenzie spread after two hours of hard riding. He decided to avoid the main trail, the one that would have brought him to the crossroads, on the grounds that there were more and more Union soldiers, not to mention refugees, clogging it up. It was indeed his intention, as soon as he'd got the gold and silver, to head West into the vast and uncluttered openness of the new frontier. He guessed it wouldn't be long before places like Turner's Holler were going to be overrun by Union soldiers.

So he headed into the wide stretches of woodlands that covered large areas of the county. Normally, when operating as a bushwhacker, he'd have sent out scouts to look out for the Union army but he didn't bother now that his mind fix had changed to that of a common outlaw whose apparent invincibility carried forward into his new occupation in life. He and his new gang were armed to the teeth. That should be enough, had been his thought as on riding out of Turner's Holler he'd spurred his horse into a gallop.

Captain Kung had shown no such arrogance on riding out away from the McKenzie farm and had sent men ahead to look for any sign of Gates still being in the area. They spotted him an hour into their ride.

'Look,' Lance Corporal Collins pointed out to Private Swallow, 'that's them.'

The two men dismounted and took cover behind a tree.

'Looks like they're heading back to the McKenzies' place,' the private stated.

162

'Yeah. Look, you ride back and tell Captain Kung and I'll keep tabs on them.'

Private Swallow did as he was told and within a short time he was reporting what they'd found to Captain Kung.

'Right,' said Kung, 'we've got him this time.'

He thought for a moment, sitting up in his saddle and looking all around him. The obvious thing was to lay an ambush for them but he didn't have enough men to be able to cover all the escape routes that would be open to Gates and his men.

'Can I make a suggestion, sir?' Sergeant Brown asked him.

'Of course, Sergeant,' was his reply.

'Why don't I take half a dozen men and get behind him. That way when he runs into you and we start at him from behind he'll think he's surrounded and by the time he realizes he ain't it'll all be over.'

Kung thought for a moment. He'd

learnt all sorts of classic military manoeuvres during the war but none of them seemed to apply now. He was used to confronting the enemy head-on in battles both knew were coming, but this was different. The bushwhackers had learnt to fight a different kind of war and he knew that to beat Gates he had to fight it the bushwhacker way.

'All right,' he said to Brown. 'We will remain mounted and let them keep on coming until they're almost on top of us and then we'll open fire. As soon as you hear gunfire open up.'

Taking six men Sergeant Brown rode off, with Private Swallow leading the way. Carefully avoiding bumping into Gates, he soon came upon Lance Corporal Collins.

'Well done, Collins,' Sergeant Brown greeted him.

'They're 'bout fifty yards over there, Sergeant,' Collins informed him by way of reply.

Brown told him and the others of the plan and they rode stealthily into position to the rear of Gates and keeping a safe distance. Like Gates and his men, they had to weave their way through now thick and then light woodland, ducking to avoid branches where they suddenly appeared as hazards and having to spread out here and there.

'As soon as the firing starts,' Brown had told his men, 'spread out into a line and start shooting. And remain mounted.'

It wasn't long before the air began to fill with lead. Gunter and Lottie, who weren't far away, heard it. They pulled up their horses and looked at one another.

'You thinking what I'm thinking,' Gunter said to Lottie, turning his head to try and gauge exactly where the sound of gunfire was coming from.

'Sure am,' Lottie replied.

He wanted to tell her to wait there while he went to investigate but he knew she wouldn't listen. Knowing that she was the one with all the experience and not him, he found himself asking her what they were going to do.

Bullets were flying all around Gates and his gang, but the bushwhackers found it hard to see exactly where they were coming from. They seemed to be surrounded but Gates couldn't see anyone. His men were taking hits but the woodland they were in was dense enough to keep them out of a direct line of barrage fire. He quickly realized the only hope of survival was escape. But in which direction? The air began to be thick with the smell of gunpowder. Firing off round after round he wheeled his horse this way and that looking for a way out of the maelstrom that was swallowing up him and his men. He decided the only way was to ride straight through the fire and hope to survive it. Half his men were down.

'Come on,' he ordered the rest, 'follow me.' And letting out a piercing rebel yell he spurred his frightened and reluctant horse into the Union fire. He rode straight through Captain Kung and his men. As ever, nothing seemed to stop him. A bullet smacked into the front jockey of his saddle and one took his hat but he made it through the line unscathed. None of his men did.

'Goddamnit!' Sergeant Brown exclaimed as he saw the back of Gates disappearing into the trees. 'Can't nothing stop that man?'

Then he called to his men to cease firing and led them to where Captain Kung was taking stock of the situation. Kung would have liked to have lit out after Gates but his soldier's mind made him stay with his men until he knew the wounded were taken care of.

'How many dead?' he asked Sergeant Brown.

'All of his, by the looks of it, but just one of ours,' Brown replied.

'Good,' remarked Kung.

'We gonna go after him?'

'What about the wounded?'

'There ain't but a few. We could leave a detail of men behind to look after them and come back for them later.'

Captain Kung looked pensive for a moment. His thoughts had filled with what had happened to Gunter's family, the slaughter Gates had visited upon them.

'All right,' he said.

He didn't know where Gunter and Lottie had made a run for and he found it hard to forget that his old school-friend had killed a man to make good his escape. What he did know, though, was that his friend was not a bad man, while Gates was. The war had made good men do all manner of bad things, while for men like Gates it had simply made greater their opportunity. He hoped that Gunter and Lottie were by now far away from anyone who might be able to point an accusatory finger at them. In fact they were not more than a mile away.

Lottie spotted Gates first. They heard the sound of a horse coming through the trees and took cover.

'It's Gates,' she said, as he came closer, his horse barely at a trot.

'So it is!' Gunter exclaimed in whispered tones.

Lottie pulled a gun. 'No,' Gunter said, reaching out and staying her hand. 'That's too easy. And, besides, he's mine.'

Gates was just a few yards away now and had not seen them. Before Lottie had a chance to reply to what he had said Gunter had lunged his horse forward into his path. Throwing himself at him he pulled him from his horse. Gates was at first stunned by what had happened but quickly recovered himself. He soon saw who it was that had jumped him. As they rolled on the ground he tried to pull his gun. Lottie watched in horror, hers at the ready. She dared not shoot though, for fear she'd hit Gunter.

Gates was the bigger of the two but Gunter was stronger. While Gates had lived a degenerate life, Gunter's had been the healthy life of a farmer. Added to this, he was mad with anger and a thirst for revenge for what Gates had done to his family. He was the first to pin his man down on his back. He brought a heavy punch to the left side of Gates's face. It all but shattered his cheekbone. Then he threw another that connected with his right side. But as he did so Gates brought up a knee that sent Gunter going head over heels. Before Gunter even landed Gates was upon him, his right hand instinctively going for his gun. He pulled it out but Gunter knocked it out of his hand. Gates tried to pin him down but Gunter grabbed his hands and wrestled him over. He was able to land another heavy punch on his cheekbone and this time it did shatter. The blow turned Gates into a raging bull and he was able to get his hands around Gunter's throat. Gunter struggled to break free but as Gates's grip tightened he began to lose consciousness. Gates might have yet again won the day had not Lottie run up from behind and slugged him with the butt of her six-gun and knocked him out. He fell spreadeagled across Gunter just as Captain Kung and his men came riding up and found them.

'Gunter, you all right?' Lottie asked him as he struggled to throw Gates off. He sat up coughing and spluttering, unable to make a reply except by nodding.

'Is he dead or alive?' Hans asked, jumping down from his horse.

'Me or him?' Gunter was able to splutter in reply.

'Him, of course,' Hans replied, standing over Gates and pointing at him.

'Alive,' Lottie replied, 'but he's gonna wish he wasn't.'

Gunter at last caught his breath and Lottie, who was at his side, put an arm around him to help him up. Hans was there too and they both got him to his feet.

'Thank you, Lottie,' Gunter said, rubbing his throat and neck. 'Reckon if you hadn't pitched in when you did he'd have killed me.'

As he spoke Gates began to come round.

'Tie him up,' Hans ordered Brown. 'And don't let him escape.'

Sergeant Brown ordered one of the men to find him some rope. Gates's face was a mess.

'What you gonna do with him, sir?' Brown asked.

'Hang him,' Gunter answered for Captain Kung.

Sergeant Brown looked from Gunter to Hans, wondering if Gunter was right.

'I don't think so,' Hans said. 'If I hang him, I've gotta hang you, too. Both of you,' he added. 'For killing the guard.'

'You gotta be kidding us,' Gunter said, beginning to cough again.

'I'm not, Gunter. I'm sorry but I gotta take all three of you to Fort Quality to go before a military tribunal. I'll speak up for you and you'll get a fair hearing. You were never part of the Confederacy, Gunter, and the North is looking to make peace with the South.

I'm sure the tribunal will be lenient with you and — '

'Supposing they ain't,' Lottie interrupted.

Sergeant Brown had finished tying up Gates and he hauled him to his feet. 'Why don't you just string him up here and now and let us go?' Lottie demanded of Hans.

'And what if I'd done that to you and Mahon?' he asked her.

'This is different. What Mahon and I did was in the war, and we was all doing it, the whole damn country. Gates here killed because it's in his soul. Mahon and I never laid a hand on a civilian, whereas he, as you damn well know, murdered every one of Gunter's family, women, children and all.'

Gates could hear what was being said about him but he was still too stunned to give a damn, except already to begin in some deep recess of his mind to plan his escape. The army understood men like him, which was why summary executions of his like had been ordered.

Men like Captain Kung, who muddied up what was a crystal-clear matter to those who knew, came in later life to wish they had followed the dictates of their elders.

Gunter listened to what Lottie was saying with a growing confusion. He wanted Gates hanged for what he did to his family but not here, not now. Had he been alone it might have been all right. But he wasn't alone any more, he had Lottie and the biggest feeling in his heart now was love. He didn't like hearing her baying for Gates's life to be ended; he wanted her to be the sweet, tender, gentle thing men living a civilized life liked their women to be.

'Lottie,' he said, pulling himself up to his full height, 'let Hans do what he has to. Let's go to Fort Quality and be done with all this. Then we can go home, go West, go anywhere and start a new life together.'

'And supposing they decide to hang you alongside Gates?' Lottie pleaded.

Gunter turned to Hans, looking for

some kind of reassurance. Hans was himself in an agony of indecision. Should he just let his friend go? And, if he didn't, what were the chances he'd be hanged just like Gates was going to be? He suddenly made up his mind.

'I would like to let you go, Gunter. I would like to do that. Who's gonna remember you killed a Union soldier? No one round here, and if they do who's gonna care? They're more likely to think of you as a hero than a murderer . . . '

Sergeant Brown, a tough and a practical man, suddenly became tired of all this indecision. Grabbing Gates, the root cause of all this trouble, and pushing him in front of him, he walked off to where the men were sitting awaiting orders. Because Gates was going to have to ride, he'd tied his hands in front of him. As he reached a group of privates he pushed Gates into the middle of them and told them to get themselves and the prisoner ready to ride. By now Gates's well-honed instinct for survival was forcing him back into full consciousness, making his intention to escape start creeping to the fore of his mind.

'You killed that guard so that I could escape because you didn't know if they were gonna decide to hang me or not and now you're gonna take that risk all over again,' Lottie was saying to Gunter. 'We've been at war, have you forgotten that? Everyone we loved has died. You gonna risk losing me now? 'Cause I sure as hell ain't gonna risk losing you.'

Gunter did not get the chance to consider what Lottie had put to him, for suddenly a shot rang out. As they turned to look where it had come from, another and then another and yet another rang out in quick succession. Gates had grabbed a gun from one of the privates and was busy wounding or killing them all, along with Sergeant Brown. In the confusion that followed he was able to grab a horse and mount it. He rode it straight at Gunter, Lottie and Hans, who were only just able to get out of its way. Gunter, though, wasted no time in mounting his own horse and quickly gave chase. Lottie was going to do the same, but Hans grabbed her arm.

'Leave him,' he said to her. 'It's his fight and this is the only way it's going to be settled.

'But — ' Lottie began to say.

'Leave him, I said. It's the only way. Help me with the men.'

12

Gates was riding dangerously fast, given the abundance of low-lying branches and the density of trees. But he was expert by now at dodging them. He would like to have reloaded the gun he'd stolen from the Union soldiers but he was unable to do so, given that he could not sit up for long enough, nor could he take his eyes off where he was going. He assumed someone would follow him, though he knew he'd done for most of the company he'd run into. Thinking of that made a smile of satisfaction spread across his face. He might yet get to lay his hands on the gold and silver buried in the McKenzies' barn.

Gunter was no great horseman but he was determined to keep up with Gates. Once or twice he was nearly knocked off his horse by low-hanging branches but so far he'd remained seated. He had a loaded gun in its holster but had not yet drawn it. He began to feel that Gates was getting away from him when the trees began to thin out a bit.

'Come on boy!' he egged on his mount, digging his unspurred heels into its flanks.

At last he thought he might get a clean line of fire. He drew his gun and fired it at Gates. He thought he had his back square in his sights but the shot must have gone wild. It did though make Gates turn round to see where it had come from and how many men there were in pursuit of him. It comforted him greatly to see there was just one. The sparse woodland ran into a clearing and Gunter began to feel he was gaining on Gates. He fired another shot but again it went wide of the mark. It didn't worry him since what he really wanted was to take Gates alive and have the satisfaction of knowing he'd dangled painfully from the end of a rope for the crimes he had committed.

Gates was now fumbling to reload his gun. He had bullets enough in the belt strap of his holster but he lost as many as he was able to feed into the chamber of his gun. Snapping the chamber shut, he turned and pointed the barrel at Gunter. Seeing him do this, Gunter lay low against his horse's neck and the bullets fired by Gates went over his head, though, in fact, coming dangerously close. Gates had emptied his chamber and was now trying to reload it again. Gunter could only think that he had somehow or other to unsaddle him.

'Come on, girl,' he sang out to his horse, 'come on!'

There was only about three hundred yards of the clearing left but Gunter had at last begun to close the gap between him and Gates. Gates's horse kept up its pace but while he fumbled to get more bullets into the chamber of his gun he drove it less. Gunter was close enough now to get a good shot at him but he hesitated and instead spurred his mount on even harder. Before Gates realized it Gunter was close enough to be able to throw himself at him and pull him from his horse. They fell to the ground with a thump and with Gunter on top of Gates. When Gates saw who it was that had unseated him he went immediately on the attack. He could still feel the pain of his crushed cheekbones and he was determined Gunter was not going to land any punches on him.

Throwing Gunter off him, Gates got to his feet. Before Gunter had a chance to get to his own feet Gates kicked him hard in the ribs. Gunter rolled on to his side and Gates landed another kick, this time in the belly. Then Gates pounced on him and pulled him to his feet. He went to punch him but Gunter recovered enough to be able to deflect a swinging right with his own right arm. As he did so he brought up a left hook which smashed straight into Gates's shattered cheekbone. In agony and momentarily dazed Gates reeled backwards and fell to the ground. Swaying somewhat and holding on to his ribs where Gates had kicked him, Gunter stepped towards him. Still swaying he pulled a gun and cocked the trigger.

'Get up,' he ordered, but Gates did no more than moan. 'I said get up,' Gunter repeated, this time drawing close enough to Gates to tap him on the leg with his foot. But as he did so, Gates's leg suddenly shot out, pulling Gunter's feet from under him. In an instant Gates was on top of Gunter, trying to get his gun. The two men began to wrestle. The gun was between them but still remained held firmly in Gunter's grip. Gates, realizing he was in a dangerous position, tried to grab Gunter's right arm and pull it away.

He had almost succeeded in doing so, when a shot rang out. For a moment both men became perfectly still. The look in Gates's eyes told all. The main artery in his stomach had been blown apart and within seconds was letting his body's lifeblood flow away. Feeling the blood soak his legs, Gunter pushed him away from him. As Gates fell on to his back he saw the last flicker of life disappear from his eyes. It was not a hanging, he thought to himself, but it was a death and that would suffice.

He decided to leave Gates's body where it was to become food for vermin and vultures. There was a stream nearby and after drinking his fill of its cool waters, he washed away Gates's blood, thinking, as he did so, that for him now the war was well and truly over. He had killed the guard, he knew that, but so many people had died and he would try and make up for it with the rest of his life.

He found Lottie where he'd left her, helping to tend the wounded. He was glad to see that the wound Sergeant Brown had received had not been fatal. The survival of Brown became fortunate for them all. As Lottie and Gunter embraced he struggled to his feet and went over to where Hans was standing.

'Sir,' he said, in between stabs of pain. 'I been thinking and it seems to me that if you have the authority to order summary execution in the field, you must also surely have the power to pardon. I mean it has to be, don't it?'

Hans looked his sergeant in the eye and then looked over to where Lottie and his friend were still locked in an embrace. It seemed to him that what Brown had said was a piece of sound logic. Gunter was a good man. If America was going to heal itself, it needed men like him. The war was over and he had killed a man, yes. But these were confused times. Had he not also saved the lives of many others by killing Gates? Surely that was atonement enough.